delight
me

For all JK's Stark World, visit www.jkenner.com

PRAISE FOR J. KENNER'S NOVELS

"It is not often when a book is so amazingly well-written that I find it hard to even begin to accurately describe it . . . I recommend this book to everyone who is interested in a passionate love story." *Romancebook-worm's Reviews* (*on Release Me*)

"A sizzling, intoxicating, sexy read!!!! J. Kenner had me devouring *Wicked Dirty* ... With her sophisticated prose, Kenner created a love story that had the perfect blend of lust, passion, sexual tension, raw emotions and love." *Four Chicks Flipping Pages*

"I have read many J. Kenner's books, but this one has to be in my top 5. It was fast paced, suspenseful and HOT." *Read.Review.Repeat Blog* (*on Shattered With You*)

"With enough emotion to rip out your heart and the right amount of sexiness and intrigue to ramp up the excitement, *Broken With You* has to be one of my favorite J. Kenner novels to date." *Harlequin Junkie Blog*

delight
me

J. KENNER
NEW YORK TIMES BESTSELLING AUTHOR

M&O

Delight Me Copyright © 2019 by Julie Kenner
The Getaway Copyright © 2016 by Julie Kenner
At The Ocean Copyright © 2016, 2017 by Julie Kenner
Cover design by Michele Catalano, Catalano Creative
Cover image by crystalstock

Digital ISBN: 978-1-949925-59-3
Print ISBN: 978-1-949925-60-9

Published by Martini & Olive Books

v-2019-12-11Pa

For Denise H - thank you for loving Damien & Nikki.

Dear Reader,

IN 2012, I sat on my couch talking on the phone with a friend in New York about a hero for whom I was sitting down to write a proposal. I could picture him, larger than life, hair dark, body lean, attitude ... well, this was a guy who pretty much owned the world. The question was ... why?

I expected to spend days thinking about that, but the truth is that Damien Stark popped into my head almost fully formed. I wanted him to have a dark background with lots of secrets. He needed to be athletic, but in a long and lean sort of way, and I knew he was a tennis player. I wanted him wealthy (obviously!) but how? Soon enough, I realized he'd parlayed his tennis career into his love of science, thus launching him on a massively successful entrepreneurial career.

A man who knew power and wealth. Who'd come from a hellacious past and now craved control over his world.

I could see a lot of women falling for him. But him connecting with them? Well, for that, I needed a woman who could hold her own, but who had her own wounds and weaknesses. A woman who fit into all of Damien's craggy, rough places. Who healed him, even as he healed her.

And that, of course, was Nikki.

I never expected the success of the Stark Saga. The

first book, *Release Me*, was my first to hit the *New York Times* list. Then it went off the next week, as usually happens for first-timers. But then it came back on the following week because the response from readers was so positive. And it stayed on that list and the *USA Today* list for many weeks, with the second and third books in the trilogy both hitting the #2 spot of the *New York Times*.

Their story continued after the HEA both because I wanted the books and because Stark fans did, too.

As of this writing, there are six Nikki & Damien novels (and — not yet announced officially, so shhhh!— there is another full-length Nikki & Damien book coming in 2021). There are also twelve novellas counting this one and the holiday novella coming in 2020.

There are multiple spin-offs, including Damien's half-brother's trilogy (starting with *Say My Name*), Jamie and Ryan's books (starting with *Tame Me*), the Stark Security series, the S.I.N. series, and several Stark World standalone novels with more to come. (A full list is included at the end of this book.)

I'll keep writing in this world for as long as there are stories to tell and readers to read them. But there are other worlds—and heroes!—too. And I'm thrilled to let readers of this book be among the very first to know that in 2020 I'm launching a scorching hot trilogy with one of the sexiest, most damaged and dangerous heroes I've ever written. If you're not already subscribed to my newsletter do it now (I'll wait) because you do *not* want to miss this! Just click here.

Now dive in and enjoy the bonus content, fun quotes, and an all-new holiday novella!

LOVE TO YOU ALL,

J. Kenner
xxoo

STARK
INTERNATIONAL

February 14

Nikki —

You are my heart.
You are my soul.
You are the love of my life.

Yours,

Damien

THE GETAWAY

Some of you may remember the scene in *Say My Name* that takes place at Nikki and Damien's Malibu house. During that scene, Damien tells Sylvia that he's sweeping Nikki away for a surprise trip to New York to see a play before they head on to Brussels to a digital conference related to Nikki's work. But since *Say My Name* was Jackson and Sylvia's story, we never saw what happened in New York with Damien and Nikki … or the events that led up to it!

This short story fills that gap, and it was previously published only as bonus content in my newsletter and in my Facebook Fan Group, the J. Kenner Krew!

I've edited the content only lightly for this release!

ONE

I stand in the open front doorway, looking out at the lush green Malibu hills and the string of cars now curving through them as they disappear down our long driveway. All in all, the party was a success, I think. But then again, why wouldn't it be? It was hosted by Damien Stark. And although I might be a teensy bit biased—what with being married to him and all—I don't think there's anything that man does that he doesn't accomplish with superlative skill.

This afternoon, we'd hosted a small cocktail party to celebrate the Resort at Cortez, a Stark Vacation Property project that is back on track after the loss of its original architect. He'd been replaced with Jackson Steele, a world-renowned architect who also happened to be Damien's first pick for a similar resort—and who'd soundly refused to sign on when Damien offered him that project.

I'm not entirely sure why he'd changed his mind,

but considering the way he was looking at Sylvia—my friend and Damien's assistant—I have a pretty good guess.

I consider that possibility as I watch them drive off in Jackson's sleek, black Porsche, then continue to linger in the doorway as I wait for Damien to return. He'd walked Evelyn out to her car, wanting to discuss something about the PR plan.

I can't see them from where I stand—Evelyn had parked around the side of the house—but after a few moments, I see her Mercedes convertible pull into view. She waves at me, but doesn't slow as she continues down the long drive to the property gate.

A few moments pass, and I consider going back inside. But I can't bring myself to do it. All day we've been surrounded by people, and now that it is just the two of us, I want to wallow in the pleasure of having claimed this man. I want to watch him rounding the side of the house. I want to see the possessiveness with which he approaches it, knowing full well that he owns the property, the house, and everything inside it.

Including me.

I want to see the heat that will flare in his eyes when he sees that I'm waiting for him, and I want to feel the brush of his lips on mine when he kisses me.

I want it—and Damien doesn't disappoint.

The moment I see him, I feel the breath catch in my throat, his impact upon me no less intense after having been married now for years. He walks with a casual confidence, his body straight and strong, his chin high. He radiates power and control, but at the same time there is an easiness to him. A weekend quality that suggests that even though he can command a boardroom, he is equally skilled on a tennis court or the ski slopes.

Or in a bedroom.

I shiver, thinking about his particular skills in that area, and when his eyes meet mine and he flashes that slow, easy smile, I'm certain he knows exactly what I'm thinking.

"Why, Mrs. Stark," he says, sliding one hand around my waist and pulling me to him. "You look like a woman with something on your mind."

"I am," I admit. I'm breathless now, my skin tingling in response to his touch.

"Whatever could you be thinking about?"

"You," I admit, then rise onto my toes to meet his mouth. The kiss is deep, claiming, and I melt against him, more than willing to surrender to his touch.

I want to simply let go. To lose myself and the rest of this afternoon in his arms. But unfortunately, I can't. I've started my own business and I have a proposal due tomorrow for a company I'm meeting with in Brussels in just a few days. I took time out for the cocktail party since it was for Damien's work, and I'll take a few minutes to spend time with him, but then I have to get back to it. If I don't, my nerves will get the better of me.

When he releases me, I sigh. "A glass of wine by the pool?" I suggest. "And then I have to get back to work. That proposal is kicking my ass."

He chuckles and I eye him sideways. He lifts his hands in mock surrender. "Just thinking about what an extraordinary ass it is."

My lips twitch, but I bite back a retort. Still, I can't help but think about his palm on my rear, and I wish I'd said nothing at all. Now I'm really going to have a hell of a time concentrating on work.

He leads me back into the house, and we move through the first floor living area to the pool deck. There's an outdoor bar there, and he pours us each a glass of wine, and we go sit with our feet in the hot tub.

"I think there's something going on between Jackson and Sylvia," I say.

His mouth curves down. "Yeah, I think you may be right."

"You really don't like him? Why? Because he turned us down when you asked him to work on the other island project over Valentine's Day?"

Damien shakes his head. "Honestly, I'm not sure. There's something about him I don't trust. He's keeping secrets."

I look purposefully at him. "Everyone has secrets."

"True." His eyes skim over me, heating every part of me. "What secrets do you still have, Mrs. Stark?"

"None from you," I say honestly.

He takes my hand, then strokes my fingers lightly. "Not even that you're worried about Brussels?"

I grimace. "It's hardly a secret if you see it so clearly."

"Fair enough. Do you want me to take a look at your proposal?"

I do. Desperately. But I also want to know that I can build this business on my own. Damien, of course, sees that clearly, too.

"Doing it on your own doesn't mean doing everything on your own. It's perfectly reasonable for an entrepreneur to pay for a consultation."

I tilt my head. "Pay? And just how much do you charge, Mr. Stark?"

His smile is slow, easy and full of promise. "The price is steep, Ms. Fairchild," he says. "But I promise you it will be worth it..."

TWO

"I don't know, Mr. Stark," I say, as Damien's finger trails down between my breasts, leaving a trail of heat in its wake. As always, his touch has taken my breath away, and it's all I can do not to tilt my head back, sigh, and give in completely.

That, however, is not the game. And so I strive to hide the tremor of excitement in my voice. "Mine's a start-up business. I have to be very careful with my investments. How do I know your consultation will be worth the price?"

"A very good question, Ms. Fairchild." I'm wearing a flowing blue sleeveless dress, with a low-cut bodice, and though the night is warm, right now I am shivering. "Let me take you point by point through the kind of detailed and in-depth study I'd make of your proposal."

As he speaks, he's inching my skirt higher. I'd held it up when we put our feet in the hot tub so as to not get the hem wet. Now he slides it up my legs, the usually mundane brush of material against skin now wildly sensual.

"First, I'd examine every aspect of your documentation," he says, his fingertip now following the path of the skirt, so that it trails up my now-bare leg. I whimper a little as he shifts toward my inner thigh, then eases higher and higher, my pulse rising with each glorious millimeter.

"I understand how important it is for you to be confident in my thoroughness," he murmurs. He shifts as he speaks, moving into the hot tub where our feet have been resting. I gasp a little in surprise—after all, he's fully clothed in khaki slacks and a button down shirt, but my surprise soon fades against the power of the arousal that courses through me when he maneuvers in front of me and puts his hand on my bare knees. "And I promise to be very, very thorough," he adds as he eases my legs apart then slowly slides both of his hands up, up, up my inner thighs.

I groan, my breasts aching, my sex throbbing, as I crave the touch I'm certain is coming. A moment later, I feel his fingertip tease the edge of my panties, the touch so close—and yet not nearly close enough.

He eases forward, his lips brushing the side of my knee. "I'm detail oriented, Ms. Fairchild," he murmurs, as he trails soft kisses up my thigh. "And customer satisfaction is my number one concern."

My skin is on fire, my pulse pounding. "Damien," I whisper, but my voice is barely a moan, and I'm not certain he hears me since instead of responding he instructs me to lie back. I obey, lowering myself until my back is on the pool deck and my gaze is on the sky.

Between my legs, Damien eases the crotch of my panties aside. He's moved closer, and I feel his breath on my sex, and sparks of electricity ricochet through me. My mouth is dry. My nipples hard against the thin material of my dress. And when he closes his mouth on me, I arch up, gasping and needy. "Please," I murmur. "Damien, please."

He doesn't answer. Not with words, anyway. But his tongue laves me, his fingers thrusting deep inside me. I arch up, wanting more. Wanting him to strip me naked and take me hard right there. I want to demand it, but I'm so overwhelmed by the sensation of his mouth on my clit and his fingers deep in my core that I can barely remember my name.

I grind against him, aroused by the scratch of his beard stubble against my tender skin and by the soft sounds of satisfaction he makes. He pulls his mouth away for just an instant to whisper, "As I said, I'm very thorough, Ms. Fairchild. Now come for me, baby. I want to taste you when you come."

His words are like the final caress, pushing me over the edge. I explode, shattering beneath the stars, my body wracked by a pleasure so intense it mimics pain. And when it passes—when I glide gently down to earth —Damien is on top of me, his body wet from the hot tub, his mouth on mine.

He kisses me deeply, and I cling to him, sated and yet wanting more. With Damien, I always want more.

"Take me inside," I whisper.

"Why Ms. Fairchild," he replies, his dual-colored eyes dancing. "I believe we have a business transaction. Assuming you find my services satisfactory?"

"Very."

His grin is slow and very sexy. "In that case, let's go take a look at your proposal. And then, my dear Mrs. Stark, I want my payment in full."

THREE

True to his word, Damien helps me tweak and revise my proposal. It's a longer process than it needs to be, because he pauses between suggestions, standing behind me so that he can see the computer screen and cupping my neck as he reads, the heat of his palm distracting me and shooting all the way down to fire between my legs. Sometimes, he slides his hand down over my shoulder to cup my breast, and I find myself biting my lower lip and moaning, filled with a delicious, needy anticipation.

But I'm a strong woman, and I'm willing to wait for what I want—and what I want is both of us desperate and needy. Not to mention a kick-ass proposal, of course.

We end up working late into the evening, but we don't finish, and though Damien pulls me close to him once we are both naked in bed, when I shift against him with undeniable purpose, he only holds me close, but makes no move for anything more than this delicious, provocative, unsatisfying touching.

"Damien," I murmur, wanting more.

"Oh, no," he says. "I wouldn't dream of asking for payment until the work is done."

I roll over, then straddle him, my sex hot and needy against the lean, hard muscles of his lower abdomen. "I don't mind making an advance payment," I murmur breathily. I shift, then bite my lower lip in response to a trill of sweet pleasure that courses through me.

I'm wildly turned on, and I know that he is too. I can tell from the way his breath is coming as uneven as mine. From the way his dual-colored eyes seem to draw me in, pulling me deeper and deeper into a wild, demanding neediness.

Most of all, I can tell by the fact that with each subtle shift of my body my ass brushes up against his rock hard erection. And with each infinitesimal touch, I see the heat building in his eyes.

"You should at least get a down payment," I murmur. "Seems like a dubious business practice to provide a service entirely on faith."

"It's not just faith," he says. "I'm an excellent judge of character, and as far as I'm concerned, you're an excellent credit risk."

I narrow my eyes, then bend lower, sliding my ass down to tease his cock even as my lips brush light over his chest. I feel more than hear his murmur of amusement.

"Nice try, Mrs. Stark," he says. "But I assure you,

your credit is just fine here." And with that note of finality, he grabs me under the arms and tugs me forward, then rolls over so that once again I am on the mattress instead of on top of him. He kisses me soundly, with just enough of a tease to make my pulse skitter and my body fire.

"Tomorrow," he says firmly. "Tomorrow we'll finish the proposal. And then I promise I'll take my payment in full," he adds, drawing his finger down between my breasts and down, down, down to my pubic bone, and then lower still until his finger flicks lightly over my clit before he pulls his hand away with a teasing, knowing smile.

I glare at him, but my heart isn't in it. Because if I know one thing for certain, it's that Damien is always true to his word—and if he promises I'm going to like it, then I don't doubt at all that whatever he has planned is going to be spectacular.

FOUR

I tap my foot nervously as Damien flips through the pages of my revised proposal, a half-eaten plate of pancakes beside him. I'm sitting across the kitchen table from him, trying to gauge his reaction by his face. But Damien is an expert in the boardroom and at the poker table, and I haven't got a clue what he's thinking.

The kitchen is on the third floor of the Malibu house. Originally designed for caterers to use when we entertain, it has morphed into the heart of our home. It's in here where Damien makes breakfast—because if I'm in charge of breakfast we have cereal or bagels. It's here where we share coffee in the afternoons. And it's where I chat with friends while I put together a tray to take outside by the pool.

I don't think I've ever once used the commercial kitchen that's down on the first floor. But this little area is cozy and comfortable, and it's one of my favorite places in the house.

Or it usually is. Right now, it's an unsettling room. I don't like waiting—I never have. And though I know that Damien is going to make my proposal better, my fear is that he's going to tell me that I've entirely missed the boat. That I don't understand my business or my market and that I'm in way over my head.

Honestly, it's not an unreasonable fear. I'd always planned to start my own business, but I was thrust into doing it much faster than I'd intended after I lost my last job because of the scandal that arose when the tabloids learned that Damien paid a million dollars for a nude portrait of me.

So, yeah, I'm nervous. Not about what Damien will think of the proposal, but that he'll say I'm not ready.

All I can do is wait, though I admit I'm not doing it very patiently. I tap my foot and sip my coffee, the dryness in my mouth making it bitter.

I reach for the creamer, then stir some in, the spoon clacking against the sides of my favorite coffee mug. That, at least, gets a reaction. He looks at me, and one brow rises very slowly. "Distracted, Ms. Fairchild?"

I make a face and point to the pages. "Finish," I order, lifting the mug. "Or are you just torturing me?" I add before taking a sip.

"Oh, torture is definitely on the agenda," he says, with so much heat that I almost choke on my coffee as my mind fills with all sorts of decadent images. "But the good news is that I'm done," he adds as he puts the last page of the proposal face down on the table.

"And?"

"And you did an amazing job."

The relief that sweeps through me is like a physical thing. "Really?" I hear the lingering worry in my words.

"Cross my heart," he says, and I slowly smile as I let myself believe him.

He holds out his hand. "Come here."

I don't hesitate, and he settles me on his lap, his arm around my waist and his body shifted slightly to the side so that we can both see the pages. "Your intro is dead on," he says. "In fact, the entire overview is perfect. But I have a few suggestions for when you get to your timeline and the description of the various phases of implementation."

I nod, shifting into work mode even though that's not easy when I can feel the hard muscles of his thighs beneath my legs and rear. And when his arm around my waist is so distracting.

"You see this?" he asks, pointing to a chart I'd inserted, and it takes all my concentration to focus on my projections and not on the way his breath is teasing the back of my neck.

He finishes his comments, wrapping up with, "None of that is absolutely necessary, though. This is quality work even without those tweaks. But I want you to feel like you got what you bargained for, especially now that I'm going to demand payment."

"Are you?" My body tightens in that familiar way in response to the heat in his voice. I shift in his lap so that I can see him better, and an additional punch of arousal cuts through me when I see the hungry way he's looking at me.

"I considered waiting until this evening," he says. "Taking you out. Undressing you in the limo. But now that I have you here..."

I have to swallow the knot of anticipation in my throat. "Don't you have to get to work?"

He flashes a smug smile. "Interestingly enough, I can be late. What with being the boss and all."

His words are cavalier, but Damien is never cavalier about work, so I know that means he has no meetings today.

I smile. "That's good news. As it happens, I don't have anything pressing at my office, either." I'm sitting with one hand on the table, and I shift the other from my knee to his crotch, then bat my eyes innocently. "And I'm the kind of women who likes to pay her debts right away. I don't like leaving a balance outstanding."

His cock stiffens under my hand, and I feel the rhythm of his breath change. Slowly, his hand that is supporting my back moves beneath my T-shirt. His palm is warm against my skin, and I close my eyes as sparks of awareness crackle like electricity over my skin. I'm not wearing a bra, and my nipples tighten against the thin cotton.

For that matter, I'm not wearing any underwear at all. I'd simply pulled on a pair of sleep shorts and this old college Tee when I'd padded in here for breakfast. Now I squirm a little on Damien's lap, a silent demand that he do something about the heat pooling between my legs.

"Shhh, baby. Be still for me," he murmurs as one hand strokes gentle circles on my back, and his other hand settles on my thigh. He trails his fingertips higher and higher until he reaches the hem of the shorts. Then he simply traces the hem until I'm so turned on and desperate that I have to bite my lip to keep myself from demanding that he slip his hand inside the shorts. That he stroke me.

That he make me come.

But I don't want to beg. On the contrary, I want to submit.

This is payment, after all. And I'm willing to let Damien take any price he wishes. Especially if part of that price is driving me insane with desire.

"I like this," Damien says, as he slides his hand up inside my shorts and finds me slick and ready.

"Do you?" I ask, I press my hand more firmly over his erection. "Because so do I."

"Naughty," he counters, then surprises me by easing his hand out of my shorts, then slipping his arm under my legs so that he can scoop me up in a fireman carry. I squeal with surprise, then suck in a breath in anticipation as he puts me down on the kitchen table and orders me to lie back.

I comply, my body trembling as I imagine what's coming. The passion in his touch. The fire in his caress. And all the wicked possibilities.

He's positioned me so that my rear is at the edge of

the table, and my feet are on the chair in which he was just sitting. His eyes meet mine, and then slowly—so painfully slowly, he lets his gaze roam over me. A heated inspection that leaves my body tingling in its wake. My swollen lips. My erect nipples, tender against the cotton of my Tee. My abdomen, the muscles quivering as his gaze moves lower and lower with all the sweet intensity of a caress.

He hasn't moved. He certainly hasn't touched me. I'm still fully clothed. But the moment that his eyes dip between my legs, my core tightens and my clit throbs.

"Damien," I murmur. "Please." I want his touch. His hands. His kisses.

"Oh, yes, baby," he says, pushing the chair away as he eases in between my legs. "It is definitely time for you to pay up..."

FIVE

The edge of the table presses into my thighs, and the surface is hard beneath my back. In truth, there's not a damn thing comfortable about being splayed out on hard, wooden tabletop. In reality, though, I'm perfectly positioned to reach heaven. And right now, I'm pretty sure that my husband holds the key to those pearly gates.

"That's it, baby," he says, gently urging my legs apart as he drops to his knees. I lift my head, but he makes a *tsk* noise and nods. The instruction is clear— I'm to lie flat on my back. I consider keeping my eyes open just because I can, but I'm not interested in a view of the ceiling. I'd much rather look at the image of Damien in my mind. And not just an image, but a movie. One in which my fingers aren't flat against the tabletop, but twined in his raven-black hair. An erotic film, where his lips brush the soft skin just above my knee, making me moan as his kisses travel higher and higher.

The pictures in my mind become more vivid as Damien does exactly that, and my body tightens as I feel the delicious scrape of his beard stubble against my inner thigh. I bite back a sigh of pleasure as I imagine the way he looks on his knees with his head between my legs, his lips slowly tracing a path higher and higher until he is so, so close. And, frankly, so am I.

"Damien," I whisper, my voice full of want. His mouth is still on my inner thigh, his cheek brushing intimately against me as his hands grip my legs to hold me steady. He's teasing me, I know. Driving me purposefully crazy. And when I raise my hands to my breasts because I'm craving more, his lips break contact and he says one simple, clear word—"No."

"Please," I protest. "Damien, please."

"Please?" he repeats, his voice teasing. "But, baby, that's exactly what I'm trying to do."

I whimper and his soft chuckle washes over me. "Hands at your sides," he orders. "I'm the only one who gets the pleasure of touching you right now."

I start to reply, but he takes my hips and pulls me further toward him, the motion so startling it steals my words. I'm balanced precariously now, open and vulnerable and so damned turned on.

And, of course, Damien comes to my rescue. Still on his knees, he sinks back down, then rests my legs over his shoulders. Once again, I can see nothing, but I don't need to. Right now, all I want to do is feel — and, oh my God, there is so very much *to* feel. My entire body is alive with a fire sparked by Damien—a fire that continues to rage and crackle through me as he pushes aside the crotch of my sleep shorts and closes his mouth over my clit.

I'm fully clothed—more or less—and yet right now I feel naked and hot before him. Like a meal laid out for his pleasure, and I can't deny that the thought is as erotic as his touch.

I'm his to take however, whenever he wants, and the fact that he's taking me here on the breakfast table is as much a turn-on as all the times he's made love to me with flowers and candles. Or, for that matter, with silk ropes and blindfolds.

I squirm against his mouth, wanting not just more but *everything*. I'm lost, swept away by the moment, lost in the intense passion of my love for my husband. And what makes it even better is that I know he is, too. I am his, yes, and that simple fact arouses both of us. But Damien is equally mine, and I revel in the deep, hot feminine power that comes from loving a man like Damien Stark.

Slowly, his hands slide up over my sleep shorts, then under the hem of my Tee. His mouth is still working its magic, and my sex clenches in anticipation of what is to come, and a small storm of electrical shocks make me tremble with the precursor of what will surely be an astounding orgasm. But then he gently tugs his mouth away, allowing the cool air to caress my bare sex. I sigh, regretting the loss of his mouth and tongue against my sensitive skin, but at the same time, I'm anticipating what is to come. *Damien.* All of him, hard and hot and deep inside me. So wild he scoots me across the table and the dishes clatter off and onto the floor.

"Yes," I murmur. I'm so ready, and I close my eyes as he stands and leans forward so that his hands cup my breasts as he lightly kisses me.

"Did you like that?" he asks, and something in his voice makes me open my eyes.

"Yes," I say honestly, but the word comes out as a question. And Damien, damn him, just grins.

"I'm glad. We'll finish later."

"Later?" The sensual cloud I'd been floating on dissipates, slamming me back down onto the hard kitchen table. I prop myself up on my elbows and glare at him. "What the fuck?"

He just laughs. *Bastard.*

"Partial payment, sweetheart. I'll collect the rest later."

"Oh, really?" I sit all the way up, sliding back so that I'm firmly seated on the tabletop. "And if I decide to welch? Because I'm perfectly ready to provide payment in full right here, right now. Later, I might not be so inclined."

"Really?" He slides his hand under my hair, then presses it to the back of my neck. An instant later his breath is hot against my ear. "Then I suppose I'll just have to provide additional enticements and incentives." His tongue teases the curve of my ear, and I moan in both longing and frustration, my sex tightening almost painfully. "And sweetheart," he adds, "no fair getting yourself off. I'll take care of you when I pay up."

"When will that be?" I demand, unable to keep the pout out of my voice.

"Soon. And I promise, it'll be worth it."

Then he kisses me lightly on the cheek and heads off toward the bedroom, leaving me desperately frustrated and more than a little bit curious about what he has planned.

SIX

It takes me a moment to get my bearings, and even when I do, it feels as though I am moving through a sensual fog. I'm so aroused that even the brush of air against my skin sends electrical sizzles coursing through me, firing at my nipples, my sex. Making my body ache with an unfulfilled need.

Damien.

He's the source of my discontent. The reason behind my sensual longing.

He is the catalyst that ignited this fire in my body, a burning need that only Damien can quench.

But he, of course, is gone.

Frustrated, I slide off the table. I know that he has something spectacular planned. This is Damien, after all, and when *doesn't* he have something amazing in the works? That's doubly true on a day like today, when it's so very obvious that he's up to something— and when he's purposefully denying us.

Fueled by both curiosity and sexual frustration, I pass through the kitchen and follow his path to the bedroom. Our deal was that he would help me make the proposal I've drafted rock solid, so that I have the absolute best chance at landing a contract with the company I'll be meeting in Brussels in two days at the trade show I'm scheduled to attend.

In exchange for Damien's services, I agreed to pay in the currency he most desired. Namely, me. And that, frankly, was a deal I'd been more than happy to negotiate.

I expected to lose myself in Damien's arms. To feel the sting of his hand on my ass, the bite of his teeth on my lips, my nipples. I had gone into the bargain with my body primed for the ultimate satisfaction. Instead, he's giving me the ultimate frustration.

And while I know that my prize will come—pun *very* much intended—today I am a woman on the edge. Damien has been teasing me since the afternoon of our party when we made this wretched agreement. And I have been walking a sensual tightrope for far too long—when all I really want to do is plunge into the abyss, knowing that Damien will be there to put me back together when I break.

In other words, I'm a hot mess. Last night, Damien stirred me up, only to leave me hanging, and during the night, my own imagination fueled my blood even more. This morning I woke to find my own fingers between my legs, trying to satisfy an aching need. Wanting Damien, I rolled over, then discovered that not only was I alone, but that his side of the bed was cold.

I'd followed the delicious smells to the kitchen, certain that not only would Damien give me the verdict on my proposal, but also finally scratch the sensual itch that was on the verge of driving me mad.

He'd done the first. He'd started the second.

And then he'd left me with what can only be described as feminine blue balls.

My only consolation is that he is undoubtedly as sexually frustrated as I am.

At the moment, that's a small consolation.

I pad barefoot down the short hall leading to the bedroom. I lean against one side of the double doors and watch as Damien lifts a leather duffel off the bed, then drops it onto the floor next to another one, identical except for being slightly larger.

"Packing already? We don't leave until tomorrow." We're taking one of the smaller jets in the Stark International fleet to New Jersey tomorrow, where the Lear Bombardier Global 8000 is currently hangered. It's huge, comfortable, and at least as luxurious as the QE2 must have been for crossing the Atlantic. Only the Bombardier is much, much speedier.

From New Jersey, we're flying to Brussels where we're having dinner with various Stark division heads the evening of our arrival. The next day, I'll be at the trade show while Damien does his executive juggling act as he meets with key players on his European management teams and also attends various functions at the trade show.

None of that, however, requires packing today.

Except when I point that out, all Damien says is, "You should get dressed." As he speaks, he nods toward the closet, where I see that he's hung a short-sleeved V-neck tee along with a soft knit maxi-skirt with slits on both sides. It's my favorite traveling outfit, as Damien well knows.

I eye him suspiciously. "What are you—"

"I believe I told you to get dressed." His brows rise with the words—and mine do the same.

Interesting.

I incline my head. "Yes, *sir*." Since my head is bent, I allow myself a secret smile. *Now*, I think. *Now things are getting interesting.*

As soon as I pull the clothes down, I see that while Damien has dangled a bra on a hanger, there are no panties included in the mix. I catch his eye, then dart my gaze to the chest of drawers.

Should I grab a pair?

The tiniest, most miniscule shake of his head.

In other words, not an oversight.

The plot thickens.

I keep my expression bland, then shimmy out of my sleep shorts. I'm not wearing anything under them, either. And as soon as I pull the top over my head and drop it to the floor, I'm standing casually—and completely naked—in front of Damien. I turn slightly, pretending to study the garment, then put my finger in my mouth, sucking gently, as if I'm contemplating some intense wardrobe question.

I make it a point not to look at Damien, but I slowly draw my finger out of my mouth, then trail it down my body, over my tight nipple, down over my belly, then over my waxed sex until I'm stroking myself. And then, despite my best intentions to stay silent, I moan aloud—how can I not when it's Damien who is touching me, at least in my mind?

And then—oh, thank God, yes—it's Damien's hands I feel up on me. Damien's fingers teasing my heated skin as he stands behind me, his breath on my bare shoulders as his hand slides down, over my breasts, my belly, and then my slick, swollen core.

He touches me, and my knees almost give out. I hold onto the closet door as hundreds of sparks snap and pop inside me as his finger teases me, slipping inside me, and making my body clench as if I could keep him there, connected to me, simply by the force of my will.

Not possible though, and soon he's tugged his hand away. I whimper, and as I do, I feel his hand on my ass. Not a quick, tantalizing smack, but an agonizingly sensual stroke between my cheeks until he is teasing my ass with one finger and with the other he's pinching my nipple.

Slowly, he slips his finger past the tight muscle, and my body sings with relief as the digit enters me. I want him. There. *Everywhere.* I want nothing more than to be filled by Damien and, finally, I'm about to get my wish.

But then his lips brush the back of my ear, his breath teasing my neck. "Don't start things we don't have time to finish, or you'll be the one who suffers. Sorry, baby. But we have to go."

———

I KEEP my curiosity at bay until we arrive at the Stark Hanger, and then when I see that it is the large, trans-Atlantic jet instead of the smaller plane, I can't hold back any longer. "Okay, Mister," I say. "What do you have planned? Why are we going early, and why is the jet here?"

I'm not sure what I expect. Considering the trade show is only one day away, we can't be detouring to London for a sensual tour of underground clubs. Not that we usually do that, but Damien took me to such a club when we were in Paris once. And though things did get a little out of control—what with the obnoxious press—I have to say it was worth it, giving me a whole new perspective on just how powerful sight can be when it comes to sexual arousal. But surely there's nothing like that on the current agenda?

Then again, I'm still banking on spectacular...

Which is why I can't help the wave of disappoint-ment when he says, "I know it's inconvenient, but there are some things I have to take care of in the New York office. It's last minute, and it has to happen tonight. But this way I can hide you away in the apartment and order you to wait for me." A smile teases his lips. "Possibly tied naked to the bed."

"Oh." A shiver runs through me. Anticipation, yes. But also disappointment. As much as I subscribe to the *all things come to those who wait* school of thought, I'd hoped we were done with the waiting portion of the equation.

He strokes my cheek, then runs the pad of his thumb over my lower lip. "You know I'll make it up to you, right? And I thought I'd start as soon as we're at altitude."

He says the last with such promise that I can only nod eagerly. After all, I'm well aware of the sensual possibilities aboard that plane, and I can't help but wonder if he ordered it back to Los Angeles specifically so that we'd have the Bombardier's bedroom. But of course he didn't—he told me this crisis only just came up. Even though the jet is fast, it still takes about five hours to cross the continent. No way could it have zipped over here that quickly from New Jersey.

By the time we're on board, I'm no longer pondering the question. It's not worth the mental energy, and I'm too busy enjoying the wine and appetizers that Katie, the attendant who routinely works Damien's flights, has offered us.

Damien spends the moments before takeoff sending texts on his phone and making sure that everything is in place to make his evening as efficient as possible so that he is away from me for as short a time as he can manage. As for me, I let my mind wander, considering the idea of telling Damien not to hurry while I go see *Second Floor, Third Door on the Right*. It's a new Broadway musical that premiered only a few months ago and is getting rave reviews. I'd want to see it for the reviews alone, but I also learned that the second female lead is Kierstan Langley, the only other pageant contestant I even came close to bonding with during my horrific days in the world of swimsuit competitions and tiaras.

I say nothing, however. I know that Damien could easily wrangle me a ticket—that's what he does, after all. But I also know that he's solidly booked. And the truth is, I don't really want to see a senti-mental romantic musical without my husband beside me.

"A refill, Mrs. Stark?" I look up to see Katie standing beside me, and realize that we've reached alti-tude while I was lost in my thoughts.

I'm about to say yes, but Damien puts his hand over my glass. "That's all for now, Katie. We'll ring you from the stateroom when we'd like another round."

"Of course, Mr. Stark." She immediately leaves, closing the door between her station and the passenger compartment.

Damien turns to me, raw sensuality burning in his eyes. "You know the way, Mrs. Stark. I'll follow you shortly."

My sex clenches in response to that heated prom-ise, and my nipples are suddenly as tight as pebbles. I nod, then stand. I start to walk to the back of the plane, but the rough sound as he clears his throat halts me.

"Did you forget something?"

I turn. "Yes, sir," I say, then don't move again until he's nodded acquiescence.

It's a game with us, and yet more than a game, too. Because the truth is, I crave his control as much as he needs my submission. I need the sting of his palm to tame my own demons, and he needs the use of my body to conquer a past that too often threatens to rise up and consume him. We complete each other, Damien and I, and I sometimes wonder how I would have made it through this world if our paths had never crossed.

The stateroom is at the back of the plane past the main passenger area. It is, essentially, a bedroom fit for a five-star hotel, only with the various details necessary to ensure against disaster in the event we hit an air pocket. A bed with straps—and not just for naughty, sexy times—tables with bungees to hold items down. Drawers that require a flip of a latch to open. But all of these things are so well camouflaged that the first impression upon entering the room is nothing more than elegance.

Today, my first impression is also delight. Because there, in the middle of the lushly made bed, is a small package wrapped in silver. The box is flat, and I glance down at my ankle where I am wearing the emerald and diamond anklet that Damien bought me even before we were truly together—though it's hard to believe there ever was such a time.

When I pick up the box, I frown. Because though I had expected jewelry, there's no heft to this box at all. A delicate chain, perhaps?

Because I know Damien, I'm certain that I'm supposed to open it even before he joins me, and so I use my fingernail to slice the paper, then pull apart the halves of the box. When I do, it's not jewelry I see, but two tickets to *Second Floor, Third Door on the Right*. I gasp, my free hand covering my mouth. And I'm so delighted by the gift that I almost don't notice the handwritten note inside the top part of the box: *Bend over the bed. Stay clothed. Spread your legs. Close your eyes.*

I take a second to savor the moment, because this is what I've been wanting. The Damien who is about to walk through that door and see me. The man who heard me mention the show only one time in passing, and yet understood that it was important to me.

The man who has put on a whole show for me so that I wouldn't suspect that this added-on trip to New York was a surprise for my benefit.

The man I love and crave.

The man, I think as I hear the door latch click, *now standing beside me.*

"Thank you," I say as he walks up behind me, then cups my rear with both hands. I'm still clothed, but the skirt is thin, and I'm not wearing underwear, and the heat from his palms seems to seep into my blood. My legs are spread as he'd ordered, and it takes all my willpower not to bring my legs tight together to try to relieve some of the pressure that is building between my thighs. But that's impossible. And all I can do is revel in the growing intensity of the need that threatens to consume me.

"I don't believe I told you to talk," he says as his hands slide to the sides of my hips, then over my scars as he moves down to the slit on either slide of the skirt. Now his hands are on my bare flesh, and as he moves them back to my rear, he tugs the skirt up as well until it is bunched around my waist, leaving me still clothed, but also fully exposed to him.

"No, sir," I say. "Maybe you should punish me."

"Maybe I should," he murmurs as he slides his hand roughly between my legs, making me cry out when his fingers find my core and I realize just how incredibly sensitive and hyperaware my body is.

"Do you have any idea how much I want you? How much I love you?"

"I do," I say, because it's true. Damien has never held back. He loves me wholly. Completely. And I love him.

"I wanted to take this slow. A long seduction. A five-hour tease. But I can't. Christ, Nikki, I have to be inside you."

"Yes." My word is a plea as much as acquiescence, and I hear his zipper as he opens his jeans and frees his cock. He's rock hard, and he strokes the tip along my perineum, driving me almost mad.

"Stroke yourself," he orders. "Touch me. I want to feel your hand as I fuck you. And after you come, I'm going to lay you out naked on this bed and take you so slowly you lose your mind."

"Do you promise?" I ask, making him laugh.

"God, you're so wet." His cock is teasing my core, one hand at my waist as he guides himself to my center with the other hand, telling me he's trying to go slowly, but he's not sure that he can.

As it is, he manages, though it's torture for us both. That, of course, is the point. And as he's moving in and out of me in slow, teasing motions, my body stiffens, my need so intense that I can't hold back the cry—the plea —to please, please, please fuck me.

And Damien, thank goodness, doesn't hesitate. He buries himself in me with one deep, intense thrust, then closes his hand over mine, our fingers teasing my clit together as he fills me—deeper and deeper, his arm around my waist keeping our bodies in a tight rhythm as he claims me.

It begins as sparks, as the orgasm so often does with me. Little fireflies in my blood that grow and change and sparkle until finally blossoming into pyrotechnical delight in an explosion so mind-blowing that I often wonder how I can be whole again after what Damien does to me. But I always am, and now, when my knees go weak and I start to sink, he scoops me up and puts me gently on the bed before climbing on beside me.

I manage a half-hearted grin. "We're both still dressed."

"I'll take care of that very soon," he says. "Trust me, baby. I'm just getting started."

I sigh with pleasure, then take his hand. "Damien," I say, my fingers twining with his. "Before you spend the next few hours making me lose myself in a sea of orgasmic bliss—and before we land and you spoil me rotten with the play—"

"And I'm taking you backstage."

I mentally swoon.

"Thank you," I whisper. "But it's just—well, I want to tell you—"

"What?"

"I love you." The words seem heavy, as if the import of them is so great I can barely get them out.

His smile is slow, his eyes more tender than I think I've ever seen. "Do you think I don't know that?"

"I know that you do," I say. "Maybe that's why it's important to say it." I swallow back the ridiculous threat of tears. "I don't ever want to take us for granted. Not anything about us."

"You won't. *We* won't."

"Thank you for erasing a little bit of the worry about Brussels, too," I say, then flash an impish grin. "I haven't had a moment to think about it during the flight, and with everything you have planned for tonight, I won't have any time to be worried then, either."

"And I intend to keep you just as busy on the transatlantic portion of our trip tomorrow." The heat in his voice leaves no mistake as to what exactly he means.

"I'm exceptionally glad to hear that."

He lifts our joint hands, then kisses my knuckles. "Seriously, baby, you have no reason to be nervous. You're going to do great."

I smile—a genuine, confident smile. "I know I am." I meet his eyes, basking in the love reflected back at me. "How can I not, with you on my side?"

FAVORITE QUOTES

You'll find favorite reader quotes scattered throughout the book! Enjoy!

And don't hesitate to share your favorite quotes on social media! Be sure to tag me (@juliekenner on Instagram) if you do!

"Possess. Have. Hold. Enjoy. Control. Dominate. Pick your verb, Ms. Fairchild. I intend to explore so very many of them."

-Release Me

"Everything I've built? All my companies? All my billions? They have no value compared to you."

- Complete Me

SEXY TEXT

A fun and sexy text from another Christmas novella,
Unwrap Me!

did you touch yourself without me on the phone? Without my voice in your ear? Did you think of me and make yourself come? Did you deny me the pleasure of hearing you moan? Of hearing you call my name as you go over? Tell me, Nikki Did you slide your fingers into your sweet cunt and imagine it was me?

Are you touching yourself now?

No.

But you want to.

Naughty girl.

Maybe I like naughty.

I like it too. Soon, baby. I'll be there soon. Until then, imagine me, touching you.

iMessage   Send

"There is no one else who has the power to tear me apart the way you do, Nikki. No one else who can reach in and squeeze my heart. You are my world, Ms. Fairchild, and I love you desperately."

- Take Me

"And as for me, there is nothing that I would not trust with Damien. My property, my soul, my heart. My life. They are his, and I know that he will treat them well. "

-Seduce Me

AT THE OCEAN

Chapter 1 (The Beach) is fun bonus content I wrote in 2016 —long before Nikki and Damien had kids—for a promotional newsletter in advance of a 2017 beachside conference! Later, in 2017, I wrote The Hotel as bonus content in my newsletter.

(Don't miss out on more bonus content! Subscribe now!)

The cool ocean breeze caresses my face as I sip coffee on the back patio of the Malibu bungalow that Damien recently built for me. It's fall, and the air is crisp and clean. I'm in a thin nightgown, and goose bumps rise on my bare arms. I hug myself in defense against the chill as I look out over the beach that is the backyard and the waves crashing against the shore, so close I can feel the spray on my face.

It's been a hell of a week.

Nothing horrific, thank goodness. No family drama. No threats from outside. None of the kinds of things that, not so long ago, would have made me curl up into a ball. Or, worse, would make me crave the sweet release of a blade against my skin. Just a tiny cut to release the pressure. Just enough so that I could go on.

This wasn't that kind of a week. It was just busy. Just hard. Too many meetings and too many projects. A good problem to have, I suppose, but I'd managed only about four hours sleep each night. And since my husband, Damien, had been away from home on a two-week long review of various Stark International subsidiaries, I'd had no real incentive to leave work early. The house is just too damn empty without him.

He's back now, though. He'd come yesterday and I'm happy to say that my lack of sleep last night had nothing to do with too much work.

I stand and stretch, enjoying the soreness in my body, remembering the way he'd teased me, stroked me, claimed me. With a sigh, I lean against the railing, looking out at the ocean as I remember the way I'd exploded in his arms with at least as much force as the waves crashing against the shore below.

"Now that is a lovely sight."

I don't turn around, but I do close my eyes, letting the warm sensuality of his voice caress my skin. My lips curve into a smile, and I feel my nipples harden beneath the thin nightgown, my body now hyper-aware and craving his touch. "I woke up alone," I say. "That just doesn't seem right."

"I had a quick errand to run. But now I suppose I'll have to make it up to you."

"I guess you will," I say, unable to keep the tease—and the desire—out of my voice.

I continue to gaze out the Pacific, even though I want nothing more than to turn and see him. I don't need to, though. I've memorized every line of his face. The strong jaw, so full of strength and power. The wide mouth that projects a delicious sensuality. The dark hair that will, this morning, be tousled from the wind, giving him the look of a man who commands not just a boardroom but the elements themselves.

And, of course, those brilliant, dual-colored eyes that have seen me so well from the first moment we met.

I close my eyes, fighting the urge to turn and look at the man I love. Instead, I listen to his footsteps on the wood, then the rustle of paper as he puts what is undoubtedly a bag of my favorite croissants on the small stone-top table. I feel the caress of his palms on my bare shoulders and the brush of his clothing against the diaphanous material of my gown.

I sigh and lean back as his arms surround me and hold me tight, as his mouth bends to my ear and I realize I'm holding my breath in anticipation of his touch. "I have something for you," he whispers, even as his fingers tease up the hem of my nightgown to slip beneath and find my core.

I moan and lean back against him, willingly losing myself in pleasure as he strokes me, teases me. How many times has Damien touched me this way, bringing me right to the precipice, and then taking me all the way to utter, soul-rendering joy? "Damien." His name on my lips is like a prayer, a wish, a sacred vow. "Please," I beg, as he uses those miraculous fingers to stroke me while his other hand teases my breast. "Yes, oh, yes, please."

But my husband can be a cruel man, too, and today, he simply brushes his lips over my ear again, then pulls his hands back so that he can step away, leaving me needy and hungry and wild with anticipation.

"You need some lessons in how to satisfy your wife, mister," I say grumpily, still facing the beach.

He just laughs. "Do I?"

"I'll find a Learning Annex class," I say archly. "Definitely a fail on your part."

I turn to face him. He is as exceptional in person as he was in my mind, and just seeing him takes my breath away. *How*, I wonder. *How is this perfect man really mine?*

"Mmm hmm," he says, clearly not believing my assessment of his failings. He takes a step toward me, then another until my gown is brushing his jeans and T-shirt. "Is that a challenge?"

"Maybe..." My sex is throbbing merely from his proximity.

"How ironic. I have a challenge for you, too. Win, and I promise I'll spend the entire weekend working to make sure my wife is one-hundred percent satisfied."

"And if I lose?"

He chuckles. "Then I'll be the one who's satisfied." He leans in and brushes his lips over mine. "I think it's fair to say that's a win-win."

Considering that nothing turns Damien on more than turning me into a melting ball of passionate goo, I have to agree completely.

"All right," I say. "What's the challenge?"

His grin is full of the promise of sex and sin as he moves to the table, then returns to hand me a small envelope that was hidden behind the white bag from the bakery.

I frown, curious, as I open it, then pull out a small card with what looks like GPS coordinates on it. "What...?"

He just lifts his hands. "That's part of the challenge. Figuring out *what* is the challenge."

I narrow my eyes, but know better than to protest further. I squint at the card again—and then it hits me. "Mr. Stark, you aren't nearly as smart as you think you are."

"Oh, but I promise you I am."

I just toss him a lofty laugh over my shoulder, then hurry into the bungalow to throw on yoga pants and a T-shirt. And, of course, to grab my phone. It's going to be essential for this game.

"I think you've been hanging out with Ronnie too much," I say as I hurry back onto the patio and down the wooden stairs to the sand. Ronnie is our niece, and she's become obsessed with *Pokémon Go*. And now my husband is sending me on an adventure, too.

I can only imagine what I'll find...

I didn't bother with shoes, and the sand is cool against my bare feet. Damien is behind me, and I wait for him to catch up, then I grab his hand, laughing with delight. I love tech and we both love science, so this is about as perfect as a game can get. He'd left the degree, minute and second symbols off of the coordinates, but it's still easy enough to see where they were meant to go. I input the numbers from the card into the GPS on my phone, and soon I've released Damien's hand and am sprinting toward a large rock that is a focal point of this stretch of beach.

The sand shifts beneath my feet as I run, and the cold Pacific surf reaches out for my ankles. I drop to my knees when I reach the rock and start scouring the area, but I see nothing. After a moment, Damien is by my side, the corners of his mouth twitching with amusement.

"A rock?" I say, holding in laughter. "You've arranged for an encounter at a rock? Because I'm not sure my comfort level with exhibitionism runs that high."

"Doesn't it?" he asks, standing behind me and running a finger down the back of my neck, sending a hot wire of desire all the way through me. "Too bad."

I press my lips together to hold back a moan. I know he's teasing me, but right in that moment, with his touch and that tinge of commanding power in his voice, I'm quite certain I'd do anything he asked.

"An encounter might be on the agenda," he murmurs, hands now caressing my shoulders, "but we won't know for sure until you finish the challenge." He bends and presses a kiss to the top of my head. "But baby," he says, his voice filled with heated promise, "I need you to hurry."

I swallow, then force my lust-muddled mind to focus. I'm certain the numbers were coordinates. I'm certain we're in the right location. And since there's nothing here except a rock, I'm also certain that whatever I'm looking for must be buried.

I shift so that I'm sitting on my rear, my yoga pants getting soaked as I ponder. Damien wouldn't put something for me where the water might wash it away. Which means that whatever is there is buried on the side of the rock away from the ocean. But the rock is big and the coordinates aren't precise, so I'm going to have to dig a long trough and hope I hit the spot.

Unless he's left me another clue.

Fortunately, once I'm on my hands and knees on the other side of the rock, I see that he's done exactly that. There is a small heart carved into the rock, still white because it hasn't yet been weathered away. And inside the heart, written very clearly, is N + D. An arrow intersects the heart at an angle, and I follow the direction with my eyes, note where it's pointing, and dig.

And less than a minute later I uncover a small metal box. I grin up at Damien, completely proud of myself, and find him smiling back at me. I open the box, and inside I find a large brass key resting on a small velvet pillow.

"Another challenge?" I ask. "Another game?"

"There might be games," he says, helping me to my feet. "There will definitely be play." His hands slide around me, one palm behind my neck, the other cupping my rear. "And I'm quite certain we'll both enjoy it very much."

"Damien." His mouth is on my neck, and his name is little more than a moan. "What does the key unlock?"

"A room," he says. "In a very exclusive, very intimate hotel." He pulls back to meet my eyes. "You've had a stressful week. So I'm taking you away for a weekend of relaxation, pampering, and a few more games. So tell me, Mrs. Stark, do you want to shut out the world with me?"

"I do," I whisper as I melt in his arms, because to that question the answer will always be yes.

"Oh, no, Ms. Fairchild," Damien says as I roll over on the bed, shifting my weight so that I can sit up. "I want you exactly the way you were."

"Do you?" There is a tease in my voice as I turn onto my side, my head resting on the down-filled pillows, my legs together, and my knees pulled up to my chest. I smile as I take in my husband's perfect body. Naked, firm, and oh-so-tempting. He may not have played professional tennis in years, but you couldn't tell it from looking, and now my eyes trail over the lean, sculpted muscles that my fingers itch to caress. "What more could you possibly want from me, Mr. Stark?"

It's a legitimate question. We've been in the charming penthouse suite of this secluded Beverly Hills hotel for the last three hours. He'd brought me here after leading me on a treasure hunt, the prize of which was the key to this room.

I'd been working like crazy and he'd been traveling, and this surprise getaway was at least as wonderful as any present Damien had ever bought me. We'd come in the limo, had lunch on the rooftop, then returned to this room—and to Damien's plans for the rest of the day.

Now, my body is deliciously, wonderfully sore. I've been worshipped, fucked, and used in all the most sensual ways since the first moment we arrived. If he were to tell me now that all he wants is for me to fall asleep in his arms, I would be disappointed, but undeniably satisfied.

But it is the wolf-at-the-door look in his eyes that lets me know that sleep is the last thing on his mind. "What more do I want from you?" he repeats. "So many decadent things."

He is standing beside the bed, and now he leans over to roll me onto my back. And then, with hands that move so slowly I am certain that he will drive me crazy before the afternoon is over, he caresses his way down over my waist, my hips, my thighs, before gently spreading my legs until I am wide open and exposed to him.

He eases onto the bed, then kneels between my legs, but he doesn't touch me. Instead, he simply looks at me. At my lips, parted now in anticipation of his kiss. At my breasts, which grow heavy under his gaze, my nipples growing harder as I imagine his fingers pinching and stroking.

Lower and lower, as his intimate inspection leaves a red-hot trail down my body, making my sex throb in anticipation of his touch.

A touch that doesn't come.

Instead, he lifts his head and meets my eyes. "Damien," I whisper, barely able to speak my mouth is so dry. "Damien, please."

"Please?" He tilts his head, his expression full of both heat and amusement. "Please, what, exactly? Tell me Nikki, what do you want?"

"You," I say fervently. "All I ever want is you."

He leans forward, his hands on either side of me, his weight making the mattress sink just a bit. "We only have a few moments before room service arrives," he says, reminding me that he'd called down to order cocktails.

"Then hurry," I demand, making him laugh.

"I'd rather be slow and thorough and make the staff wait at the door." And before I can respond, his mouth closes on my breast and I arch up, the electricity of that connection shooting from my nipple all the away to my clit. I gasp, then moan when he raises one of his hands to my mouth, his thumb stroking my lower lip. I draw it in, sucking and tasting, as he does the same, his mouth claiming my breast with equal fervency.

"Please," I beg as his free hand cups my other breast even as his mouth starts to move lower, teasing his way down my belly, then lower and lower still until his tongue is tracing a path along my pubic bone, along the soft skin between my thigh and my sex.

He's making me crazy with longing, and I shift and writhe, desperate to escape this assault, so intense that it is almost painful. "I can't," I gasp. I'm truly on a knife-edge, and it is Damien that is tormenting me.

"You can," he counters. "You will."

It's only when I realize that I can no longer squirm away from him that I realize his hands have left my mouth and breasts. He's holding my hips down, keeping me steady. Controlling me. Not just giving, but making me take. Not just teasing my clit, but demanding that I feel. That I submit. And as his mouth strokes and teases and plays me so perfectly, I fall willingly under his spell, lost in a sweet torment that is so perfect it is fragile. So incredible it is explosive.

"Now, baby," he demands. And my body obeys. I break apart beneath him, riding out the power of his touch, falling over into wave after wave of orgasmic bliss that leaves me gasping and sated, both empty and full, for what must be the millionth time that afternoon.

"Damien." His name is a whisper, but it is also a plea, and he understands exactly what I want. He eases up the mattress and pulls me close, holding me and caressing me, every stroke, every breath, telling me how much he loves me.

"You," he whispers, then kisses my shoulder. "You're my world, Nikki."

I close my eyes, relishing the moment, only to be startled back to awareness by the rap on the door.

Damien eases off the bed, and I watch as he leaves the bedroom, sliding on a robe as he does so. A moment later, he returns with a tray carrying an ice bucket, two highball glasses, and a bottle of Scotch.

As I watch, he starts to open the bottle, but then he stops and takes the lid off the ice bucket instead. He takes out a single ice cube, then holds it over my belly.

I bite my lower lip, waiting. Because I know where this is heading. I recognize the gleam in my husband's eye.

A moment later, a fat drop of water falls off the ice to land just above my navel.

Damien's eyes dip down, then back up to me. The corner of his mouth curves up into a smile.

"So tell me, Mrs. Stark. Are you tired?"

"No," I say, reaching for his free hand and pulling him close. "I'm not tired at all."

"Do you know what passion is?

Most people think it only means desire. Arousal. Wild abandon.

But that's not all. The word derives from the Latin. It means suffering.

Submission. Pain and pleasure, Nikki. Passion."

-Release Me

ANOTHER SEXY TEXT

Here's another sexy text! This one from Seduce Me!

Just arrived in Sin City. Feeling deliciously sinful. Who knows where that will lead…

I'm intrigued. Take pictures.

???

If you're naughty without me, I want to know exactly what I'll be punishing you for later.

And no underwear. When I think of you, I want to think of you bare.

Yes, sir. Whatever you say, sir.

Good girl. Meeting starting. Soon, Mrs. Stark. Until then, imagine me, touching you.

I always do.

 iMessage   Send

DELIGHT ME: A STARK CELEBRATION

A quick note from JK. I hope you enjoy this all-new holiday novella featuring Nikki & Damien!

In case you're wondering, this story fits in the chronology after the events of *DAMIEN,* but before the Stark Security Agency has been officially formed. (And if you haven't read the Stark Security books yet, what are you waiting for?

Stark Security:
Charismatic. Dangerous. Sexy as hell.
Meet the elite team of Stark Security.
Shattered With You

Shadows Of You (prequel to Broken With You)
Broken With You
Ruined With You
Wrecked With You

Now keep flipping pages for more Nikki & Damien!

ONE

I wake to the tickle of Sunshine on my nose. Not the kind that streams in through the glass doors leading from the bedroom to the balcony. No, this Sunshine is warm and furry, with whiskers that tickle my cheeks and a purr that is powerful enough to shake the bed.

Reluctantly, I peel open my eyes. The cat might be comfy and content this morning, but I'm not ready to be awake. Christmas is fast approaching, and my partner Abby and I had stayed up until three in order to get the updates for five of our gaming products out before the holiday.

"What time is it?" I ask the cat. She doesn't answer, but she does nuzzle my face, which I interpret as *breakfast time.*

I sigh, then roll over, planning to finagle my husband into handling this domestic chore. But instead of Damien, long and lean and naked, I find nothing but a tangle of sheets and a slight indention in his pillow.

Without thinking, I reach out and rest my palm on the place where his body should be. It's cold, and my chest tightens with a quick stab of fear before reality and reason win out. Nothing has happened to him. Or, more specifically, nothing has happened to him other than being sucked into the whirlwind that is two little girls.

Still, I wish that he'd woken me. My head knows it's foolish to immediately imagine the worst when anyone I love isn't exactly where I want them to be. But kidnapping rewires your brain, and now I have to work extra hard not to hold my kids so close it smothers them.

Damien, too. Though there has never been a time when I haven't held him close. Haven't drawn strength from him.

And that, I realize, is why I feel so alone this morning. I'd gone to bed worried that we'd missed something in the rollout, and those worries had grown and shifted, turning personal in my dreams. Potential failures in my job morphing into demons in my personal life. The kind of demons who sneak in around the edges and hurt your family. Your children.

The kind of demons I've always relied on Damien to protect me from. The kind that he has always known I'm able to fight myself, so long as I harness the strength inside me.

"Just dreams," I tell the cat. "Stupid nightmares."

She blinks at me, entirely unimpressed.

"Silent treatment, huh? Fine, come on. I'll feed you."

That she responds to, hopping nimbly off the bed and then prancing to the door, her tail high. She looks back at me, her head cocked as if to silently scold me for moving too slowly. I grab my robe from the back of the armchair by the door, then slip it over my naked body. I'd briefly tried to sleep in a nightshirt or sleep shorts after we adopted Lara, but it never stuck. The feel of my skin against Damien's had become as comforting as sleep itself, and neither of us had made the transition.

Knowing the force of Damien's will, I'm certain he hadn't tried too hard, but that was fine with me. We compromised by adding parenting to the mix, explaining to Lara, a very precocious four-year-old, that everybody is entitled to privacy, and that she and her sister aren't allowed in our room without knocking first. With the exception of a couple of nightmares, she's never broken the rule. And when she shared the bed with us during those horrible days of Anne's kidnapping, we of course deferred to modesty and pajamas.

Now, our bossy little girl is instilling the family rule in her little sister, making sure that Anne, now two, is completely with the program. Frankly, it's both hysterical and adorable. Though I do sometimes wonder when Anne will get to be the bossy one.

As it stands, Anne only lords over Sunshine. Who, thankfully, adores the children and doesn't scratch and yowl when either of the girls tries to dress her up for tea parties or enlist her in wild games of chase. Instead, she suffers quietly until she's reached her limit, then goes and hides under the sofa where little arms can't reach her.

"Good, kitty," I say now, my words earning a twitch of her whiskers as she undoubtedly wonders what she did to earn such praise. "Let's go find you something fishy for breakfast."

Damien was in the process of building this house when we met, and the primary kitchen was supposed to be the one on the first floor. It's a huge set-up, complete with commercial-grade everything. A Disneyland for culinary types.

In other words, it's incredible. And we don't use it at all.

Instead, the real "primary" kitchen is the small and cozy set-up off the third floor open area, just a few short steps from the hall that leads to both the master bedroom and the room that the girls share. This kitchen was meant to be the finishing and serving area for caterers. But despite the limits on its intended use, it's a fully functional kitchen, complete with a round table that is plenty large enough for a family of four. Five, counting Gregory, who's been with Damien longer than I have. Officially, Gregory is a combination butler and valet. But he's more like a house manager and, more recently, he's added the job of nanny to his portfolio.

Sunshine scratches at the pantry door, and I hurry to catch up, then refill her kibble bowl. She sniffs it, then proceeds to twine through my legs until I've opened a can of wet food and put it down next to the apparently subpar dry choice.

Immediately, she ceases loving on me, and I'm released to turn to the second-most important task of the morning: coffee.

Finally set with a steaming cup of black coffee in my hand, I make my way to the girls' room. Originally intended as a small guest suite, it is accessed from the hallway, and its longest wall abuts the master bedroom's extremely huge walk-in closet, providing some privacy despite the close proximity.

I pause in the doorway, not terribly surprised when I see that the room's only occupants are of the stuffed animal variety. I wonder if Damien has taken them down to the beach, or possibly to the tennis court so the girls can chase balls as he gets in a quick workout.

I consider getting my phone from the bedside table and simply calling him, but there's something so wonderfully sweet about knowing that he's with his daughters that I don't want to interrupt.

Instead, I head to the stairs, intending to check the first floor playroom. If I don't find them there, I'll go out to the courts. If that doesn't turn up a sign of my family, I'll get my phone and map them. Maybe I'll see that they've gone to Upper Crust, and will soon be returning with some sort of wonderfully delicious flaky pastry. A yummy Saturday breakfast before we head out to spend the day with family and friends.

A girl can hope.

But thoughts of melt-in-your mouth goodness are erased as I reach the first floor landing. I'm still yards away from the playroom's entrance, but I can hear Lara's high-pitched declaration clear enough, "More glitter, Daddy. Fairies need lots and lots and lots of glitter."

"Me glitter!" Anne's still baby-ish voice is surprisingly strong, and I smile as I pick up speed, my bare feet quiet on the cool tile floor.

I round the corner and pause in front of the open double doors of the huge bonus room that now serves as the girls' playroom. Pure joy courses through me, so fresh and bold it's a miracle the power of it doesn't cause the three heads in the room to turn and look my direction.

As if to hold in my own delight, I press my hand over my mouth as I watch Damien, his dark head topped with a Santa hat, drizzle glue onto the single filmy wing I'd managed to construct for Lara.

I'm a lot of things, but crafty isn't one of them. I'd intended to fight it out with the wire and material to make wing number two before adding the sparkles, but apparently a little girl with a daddy wrapped around her finger had other ideas.

I try to keep my lips pressed together, determined not to make a sound, but so full of joy that a bubble of delicious laughter manages to escape.

Anne squeals and scampers toward me, moving remarkably fast on her chubby toddler legs.

Lara, tall and wiry for her age, beams as she jumps

up and down. "Daddy's making my wings sparkle! Mama, come see, come see."

"I do see," I tell her, scooping up Anne and breathing in her baby-scent as Damien stands up then turns to look at me. His Santa hat sits at an angle on his raven-dark hair, and he holds his hands out to his sides, careful not to get glitter and glue on his favorite faded jeans.

I meet those amazing eyes, so uniquely his, and then I melt a little as his lips curve in that familiar, enigmatic grin. "Good morning, Ms. Fairchild," he says.

"Mrs. Stark," I counter, feeling the smile tug at my lips. I deposit Anne back on the ground and move toward him. A moment later, my arms are around his waist and my head is tilted back to look up him, so vibrant and perfect and mine.

Things haven't always been easy, especially this time of year. Between my mother and Damien's father, who would blame us if we ran screaming from the holidays? But we've carved our own way. Made our own world. And now, in the arms of my sparkle-covered husband, I can't help but think that this moment is just about perfect.

At least until I hear Lara's sharp cry of, "*Nooooo*," followed by Anne's shrill scream. All underscored by the clatter of bottles and jars and boxes tumbling to the ground along with the now-toppled table that was holding them.

TWO

"Mamamamama! Anne smooshed my wings! She smooshed them!"

Damien winced as his eldest daughter's shrill cry pierced his eardrum.

"She didn't mean to, sweetie," Nikki said, already at the table, her arms reaching out to embrace two very distressed little girls. "She grabbed the tablecloth, but she didn't know what would happen."

"But she *ruined* them." Lara blinked, clearly trying to hold back tears. Anne made no such attempt. Her little cheeks had turned red, and big crocodile tears spilled down them as she wailed.

"Hush, baby," Nikki cooed even as she stroked Lara's hair. Both girls calmed visibly, and Damien breathed in deep, his chest tight. Not out of annoyance from the accident or irritation from the children's squeals. No, what he felt was pure adoration and respect.

He'd never doubted that Nikki would make a good mother. Maybe someone else would fear that with the complete lack of a role model she'd grown up with, Nikki would have been clueless. But Damien hadn't doubted. And now his heart filled simply from watching the way she soothed their daughters.

He started to step forward in assistance, but Nikki's next words both stopped and amused him. "Daddy can fix the wings," she said. "You know how good Daddy is at fixing things."

"Not this." With her little chin shaking, Lara picked up the now-bent wing, which also happened to be covered in glue, bits of craft detritus, and far too much glitter. "You can't, can you?" She looked up, pulling him into the conversation.

"Hmm." He eased forward, crouching down in front of his daughter. "Well, you know, I think you're right. I don't think I can."

"See?" Lara scowled at her mother, her expression so like a vindicated adult that Damien almost laughed. And from the twitch at Nikki's lips, he assumed she was fighting mirth as well.

"I stand corrected," Nikki said, her voice high-pitched with amusement. "I truly thought Daddy could do anything."

"Hmm. Well, what I *can* do," he said as he transferred the little girl into his arms, "is make you an even better pair of wings."

"But that one was the bestest."

He shook his head. "That was a prototype."

She blinked at him.

"A tester. Like when you practice writing your alphabet. The more you practice, the better you get."

"Oh."

"So tonight, we'll make you new wings. And the frame will be shaped better and we'll make sure the glitter goes on just how you want it."

"And her?" Lara pointed an accusing finger at Anne, who promptly shoved her thumb into her mouth.

He glanced at Nikki. *Ideas?*

Her answering grin told him she had a plan. "You know Anne loves to be around you and Daddy. So why don't you think of a way to keep her entertained so she doesn't accidentally get in the way. Maybe with her own glitter and glue?"

Lara's lips pursed, her forehead creased with concentration. "I'll give her custrom paper. So she can make glitter stars."

"Construction," Nikki corrected. "And that sounds like a great plan. Don't you think, Daddy?"

"Best plan I've ever heard. Now why don't you help me clean the mess up while Mommy cleans up your sister. She's more sparkly than she should be."

"Sparkee!" Anne cried, thrusting her arms up and giggling, knowing by some childlike intuition that the storm had rolled over.

By the time he and Lara had set the table right and put everything back on top, Anne was tugging on his leg, only a few stray specks of glitter on her nose and in her hair catching in the light.

He squatted down, pulling each girl into a hug, then looked up to see Nikki beaming at him.

"Hello, there," he said to his wife, then added to the girls, "Should we guess what Mommy's thinking about?"

"Cookies?" Lara suggested.

"I'm not thinking anything. I'm just soaking up the view."

"So am I," he said, his eyes raking over her, enjoying the way the fluffy robe hid the soft curves he knew were underneath.

"Mmm," she said as she pulled her phone from her pocket and snapped a quick picture. "I know that tone. Behave."

He widened his eyes and tried to look innocent as he stood. "I have no idea what you're talking about."

Nikki shot him an amused grin as she looked at the phone display, her smile growing broader. "This one's definitely a keeper. The girls are clean now, but you, Mr. Stark, are even more sparkly."

"Daddy pretty!"

"Can we make stars for the party?" Lara asked. "We can put them on the tree." Their Christmas tree took up one corner of the third floor open area. They'd decided to place it near the railing so that it was visible from the first floor, which had especially delighted the girls.

"I don't see why not," Nikki said. "Every Christmas Eve party should have stars."

"And since we're hosting it," Damien told Lara, "I think we can have as many stars as you want to make."

"Yay!" Lara bounced and grabbed Anne's hands and his two daughters morphed into little girl-shaped containers of pure energy.

Nikki moved to his side and they stood there, watching the insanity that was their kids until he heard the soft clearing of a throat behind them and turned to see Gregory.

"Good morning, sir."

Damien bit back a sigh. He'd long ago given up on trying to convince Gregory to lose the formal touch. "Good morning, Gregory. Did you need me?"

"Actually, I was going to offer to fix the young ladies a snack before you go."

"That would be fabulous," Nikki said, indicating her robe with her hand. "I still need to shower and dress. You two behave," she added, pointing to the girls. She met Damien's eyes. "You, too."

"Careful, wife," he said, making her laugh as she hurried out of the room.

"That's nice of you to offer," Damien told Gregory. "But it is your day off." When Bree, their previous nanny, had left for college in New York over the summer, Gregory had stepped in to fill the nanny gap. Though originally intended as a temporary arrangement, he'd asked to keep the position in addition to his other duties. His own daughter had never had children, and he doted on the girls. But the extra work meant that the poor man surely needed his free days more than ever.

"It's only for an hour or so while you and Mrs. Stark get ready. And how better to spend my down time than with my two favorite girls?"

"I know exactly what you mean," Damien admitted as Lara clapped her hands and Anne mumbled something around her thumb that sounded like *miss her gee,* which Damien interpreted as Mr. G.

"I guess that settles it," Damien continued, glancing quickly at his watch. "We need to be out the door in an hour if we want to get there on time."

"Of course, sir."

"Daddy! Daddy, stay. Wanna make fairy wings for Mr. G."

"As tempting as that sounds, I need to check in on something at the office. But I'll be done soon and we'll go see your cousins, okay?"

"Yay!" Lara started to jump up and down, and after a quick look from Damien to Gregory to Lara, Anne joined in, apparently deciding the craziness was okay.

"And this is where I leave you," Damien said, then smiled at Gregory's faux look of horror.

The last thing he heard as he rounded the corner into the hall was Gregory's suggestion that they go to the kitchen for a snack of apple slices and cheese. A suggestion that was met by applause and giggles.

He'd spoken the truth. He did need to check in at

the office. But the person he needed to check in with, Ryan Hunter, was joining them for brunch at his brother's house.

Which meant that Damien had only one thing on his mind that needed his attention right then. And that thing was Nikki.

As he'd hoped, she was still in the shower. He could hear the water running as he entered the bedroom and turned toward the massive, contemporary-style master bath.

He'd designed it himself, with some input from his architect. Those were the days before he knew his brother Jackson even existed, which was a pity, as Jackson was one of the most skilled architects on the planet. Even so, Damien had to pat himself on the back. This bathroom was a showpiece, designed for decadent comfort.

But the best thing about it right then was the naked woman standing in the slate-tiled shower, the details of her body hidden by the fog on the floor-to-ceiling glass doors.

"Are you just going to stand there looking at me?"

He was already on edge, and her voice, low and sensual, roused him as much as is she were touching him. He stepped the rest of the way inside, then shut the bathroom door and leaned against it.

"Unfortunately, I waited too long. There's far too much steam to look at you properly."

"I guess you'll have to open the door and come in if you want a better view."

"I guess so."

She wiped away a tiny bit of fog, then peered at him. "I'm surprised you didn't think of that yourself. I thought you had a reputation as a problem solver."

"I do," he said, pushing away from the door and walking slowly toward her. "Tell me your problems."

"Well, for starters," she said, "you're out there. But I want you in here."

THREE

I use a washcloth to rub a bigger clear spot on the steamy glass, then I watch as Damien peels off his jeans and t-shirt, leaving him wonderfully, gloriously naked.

A former professional athlete, he still stays in incredible shape, and I bite my lower lip as my own body reacts in response to this view. His hard, muscular thighs. Those perfect abs. His upper arms, lean and strong.

A thin strip of hair runs down his abdomen, guiding the way to his cock, already hard. Not surprising, I suppose. I'm already wet, after all. And not just from the shower.

He meets my eyes, and the heat in his slow, almost lazy grin, shoots through me. I press my fingers to my breastbone, then slowly slide my hand down, watching his face as I go lower and lower until my body trembles as I brush my fingertip over my clit before easing my hand lower, only to stop when he softly but firmly says, "No."

I stop, but keep my hand where it is. "No, Mr. Stark?"

He crosses to the shower door in two long strides, then pulls it open and joins me in the steamy compartment. "No," he repeats, placing his hand on mine, and then guides both our fingers down until I'm stroking my pussy with him, and he's thrusting two each of our fingers inside me.

I gasp, overwhelmed by this new sensation.

"No," he continues, as if my fingers weren't already deep inside me. As if he hadn't put them there. "Not without me. Not today. Today, you do what I say." He steps closer, his erection pressing into my belly. I close my eyes, need crashing over me, making me weak.

Just a few minutes ago, he was gorgeous and sexy in sparkle-covered jeans. Now he has me naked and wet, giving me orders that I know better than to disobey. And damned if I don't adore both sides—all sides—of this man.

"Lift your arms," he orders. "And hold on to the pipe."

In addition to the two rainfall-style heads that extend from the ceiling, the shower has six jets that spray from two adjacent walls as well as one hand-held showerhead.

I follow his instructions and turn my back to three

of the jets, then lift my arms to hold tight to the topmost pipe.

"Very nice," he says, dousing a bath sponge in shower gel and slowly sudsing me up so that I sigh and melt a little under his ministrations.

His touch is gentle, almost sweet, and I let my head fall as I sigh with pleasure. A moment later, he pulls the sponge away, then steps back. I open my eyes, confused, but he only smiles as he takes the handheld shower head, sets it to a light spray, and slowly rinses me off.

He starts with my shoulders then works his way down, the water sluicing over me in a familiar fashion that, under the circumstances, seems entirely erotic. He spends extra time on my breasts, and I feel my nipples tighten, a hot wire of desire running from my breast to my sex, and as his right hand continues to move the nozzle lower and lower, his other hand fingers my breast, teasing my nipple with increasing intensity as a wild heat curls inside me.

"Damien," I murmur as he nudges my legs apart, then aims the handheld spray at my center. I wriggle my hips, wanting the spray to hit me just so, but he puts a firm hand on my waist, keeping me still.

"I want to touch you," I whisper. "Please, can I take my hands down?"

"No," he whispers, then looks up to meet my eyes. "Not yet."

I make a noise in protest, then swallow it as he

adjusts the nozzle, increasing the spray so that it now pulsates against my clit. I arch back, trying to move, the pleasure almost too intense to bear. But Damien holds me in place, and my whole body shakes as the precursor of a massive orgasm rocks me.

"Damien," I say. "Please." But damned if I know what I'm asking for. I've gone to that place of sensation and longing, and it's Damien who's led me there. And Damien who will lead me back again.

Still, he doesn't relent. But he does bend forward long enough to press his lips to my ear and whisper. "Not yet, baby. I want more."

"Then let me touch you."

He shakes his head. "More of you, Nikki. I want to see the way your skin changes as you get aroused. The way your lips part when you want me. I want to run my tongue over your nipples, so tight with need. And most of all, I want to feel your cunt tighten around me when I take you all the way over the edge."

I whimper, but say nothing.

"This isn't about me, baby. So relax. All you have to do is come for me. Can you do that?"

I nod.

"Good," he says as he slides his hand down and cups me. "Christ, you're slippery. I may have to fuck you sooner than I intended."

"Okay," I say, and he laughs, obviously surprised by my quick and heartfelt response.

"We'll see," he says, then drops to his knees. His

hands are still on my hips, and his kisses start at my inner thighs. He works his way up, his tongue flicking over my clit just long enough to ramp me up again. Then he continues upward, his mouth tasting and kissing until he reaches my breasts. He nips at my nipples in turn, his oral ministrations alternating with fingers pinching until I'm half-convinced I'll come that way alone.

Then he's standing fully upright, his fingers twined in my hair as he tugs my head back to the angle he wants before closing his mouth over mine and claiming me in a wild, deep, violent kiss.

"Now," he says when he pulls away. "Hold on, baby," he says, then grabs my ass and lifts me so that, for a moment, I'm supporting most of my weight with my arms on the jet. Then he thrusts inside me, and I cry out in both pleasure and surprise as I close my legs tight around him, both to relieve the pressure on my arms and so that I can draw him even further inside.

"Let go," he orders, and I do, moving my hands to his shoulders as he turns us in one quick move and slams my back up against the glass shower wall.

"Ease up, baby," he says as he grips me at my upper thighs. I'm trapped, held in place by the glass and by the force of his thrusts as he moves deep inside me, over and over. I grip his shoulders hard, and look deep into his eyes as he fills me, hard and deep, taking me closer and closer to the edge.

"Come on, baby. Come with me."

His words are a demand that my body obeys, shattering suddenly as if I'd gone supernova. But never once do I close my eyes or break the connection. And as my soul spins out of control, it's the intensity in Damien's eyes that brings me back again. Back to the arms of the man I love.

FOUR

It's a gorgeous December morning, the sun shining down on the stunning homes that dot the hills of the Pacific Palisades. The ocean glitters behind us, and as we go over hills and around turns, we catch small glimpses of those deep blue waters.

I glance into the Range Rover's back. Lara is absorbed with reading her current favorite book, *Don't Let the Pigeon Drive the Bus*, while Anne draws furiously with crayons in her new Christmas-themed coloring book. Neither is car sick or whining or complaining about her sibling.

Truly, the holiday season is a miraculous time.

I resettle myself in the passenger seat as Damien turns onto Jackson and Sylvia's street. When we'd first met Jackson Steele, he was living on a houseboat he keeps docked in Marina del Rey. After he and Syl got married and Jackson built this house, he'd kept the boat as an office for a while. Now, the entire operation has moved its base from New York to Los Angeles, and it's far too big a company for a boat. Instead, Steele Development is in its own building at The Domino, a retail and office complex in Santa Monica that was designed by Jackson and co-developed with Stark Real Estate.

As for the houseboat, he currently rents that to my lifelong friend, Ollie McKee. A former lawyer, Ollie recently transitioned to the FBI. More important to me, he's once again living permanently in Los Angeles, and I'll see him in just a few hours at The Domino's Winter Wonderland event.

We round a bend, and the stunning contemporary that Jackson built for Sylvia rises in front of us. Elegantly minimal, the house seems to be part of the landscape, not something plunked down onto it. The lines flow, some to the sea, some to the heavens, and the front door of glass and steel offers the only view to the driveway and the street beyond. All the other windows face the ocean.

It's unique and lovely, and I'm pretty sure it's been featured in every major architectural magazine, as have most of Jackson's designs.

Damien maneuvers into the drive and parks behind the sleek black two-seater Ferrari that he gave to Jamie years ago. I frown, wondering if that means that Ryan's sister, Moira, cancelled. I hope not. I know she's busy finishing up her Masters in marketing, but it would be a shame if she missed out on the holidays. Not to mention the fact that the girls adore her, and always beg for Moira to babysit when Gregory can't watch them.

Since Damien and I have kid-transport down to a science, it doesn't take long to get the girls unstrapped and out of the car. Immediately, they scamper to the open door and race inside to find their cousins.

Damien and I move more slowly, enjoying what has become increasingly rare alone time. "I was thinking this morning that it's a shame I didn't know Jackson when I designed the house. Ours is good. His is better."

"Ours is amazing," I counter, stating what I consider an empirical truth. "And it's not as though you two hit it off right away. There was that whole period where he thought you were as much of a devil as your father."

"Mmm," Damien says, and I'm thankful he doesn't expand on the topic. The last thing I meant to do was pull Jeremiah Stark into any holiday-related conversation. Or *any* conversation for that matter.

"Besides, it's not like you two haven't made up for lost time. So many projects, and The Domino is topping them all." The complex is not only at full capacity, it's won almost every major award for design that exists.

Stark International's Resort at Cortez—an island development—is another that added a feather to Jackson Steele's already full cap. But while Damien was personally involved in The Domino, Syl was the

Stark representative who took point and worked with Jackson on that.

I bite back a smile.

"What?" Damien asks.

"Just thinking that Syl and Jackson got together working on The Resort at Cortex. What kind of bromance did you two have working on The Domino?"

He chuckles. "The best kind," he assures me. "The kind where our wives are like sisters, our children are cousins, and where Jackson and I made up for some of those lost years when I didn't have a clue he existed."

"You did that before," I say.

"True. But we lost a lot of years. And we have a lot of time to make up for."

As if he knew we were talking about him, Jackson steps over the threshold and stands beneath the porte-cochere as we continue down the etched concrete drive toward the stunning contemporary-style home. He's younger than Damien, but like my husband, Jackson stands with a confident posture that suggests that he owns the world. His hair, as dark as Damien's, is thick and tousled, and his strong jawline is rough with beard stubble.

But it's his eyes that are his most striking feature. A vivid blue that can be either as warm as a summer sky or as cold as an arctic sea. Now, they are warm and inviting.

"I was beginning to think you dropped the kids and ran off on your own."

"Tempting," Damien says, as Jackson kisses my

cheek, then hooks an arm around each of us and guides us into the waiting chaos.

And chaos it is.

While the view of the Steele home from the front may be worthy of Architectural Digest, the interior is a screaming, writhing pit of insanity otherwise known as The Gathering of the Cousins.

"It's too early for whisky," Sylvia says, approaching with a flute full of orange liquid. "But a mimosa should take the edge off."

I take it eagerly, then follow her through the house to the back patio. The kids are ahead of us, and Lara and Ronnie, their oldest at seven, are already clamoring for the swings while three-year-old Jeffery and Anne have plunked themselves down in the sandbox.

"Should we go down?" I'm imagining little eyes stung with sand.

"Moira's there." Sylvia points, and I see the pretty dark-haired girl come out from behind the shed with a bouncy ball.

"I was afraid she skipped out on today when I only saw the one car."

Sylvia rolls her eyes. "She actually sat in the back of that thing. I have no idea how she fit. She's what, five-ten?"

"Maybe she's foldable," I say, and we both laugh.

Syl, I think, would have no trouble curling up in the back of the Ferrari. She's shorter than me, not petite, but not tall. These days, she's wearing her hair short again, and the pixie cut suits her. I originally met her when she was Damien's executive assistant. Now, Damien's right; she's like a sister, both by marriage and by friendship.

"I'm sorry Evelyn's not coming," I say, thoughts of sisters pushing my thoughts to my own mother, and then veering me quickly away. Elizabeth Fairchild may be tied to me biologically, but Evelyn Dodge is the woman who feels like my mother. And, in fact, she gave me away at my wedding. As Damien's former agent, she's been in his life since his tennis career, and I know she loves him as much as I do. More than that, she loves me, too.

"She had something she couldn't get out of. She's hoping to get free in time to see us at The Domino."

"Fingers crossed," I say, happy to be able to see her even if I won't see my father, Frank. He was supposed to play the role of Santa at the Winter Wonderland, but he's a travel photographer, and got a plum assignment that conflicted with the Santa gig.

I'm disappointed, of course, but apparently the company that booked him is paying all expenses, plus he was able to tag his own trip on at the end, allowing him to take another assignment to shoot advertising photos for a Mexican coffee plantation.

That's where he is now, somewhere in Chiapas, and I'm hoping that means I'll get coffee for Christmas.

"He'll be back for Christmas Eve, won't he?" Syl asks after I tell her all that. "The kids will be so disappointed if he's not at the gala."

The fairy wings that caused such drama this

morning are part of a fundraising gala for the Stark Children's Foundation, an organization that provides assistance to abused and neglected kids. At five p.m. on Christmas Eve, a gaggle of kids from three dance schools that provide sponsorships to the SCF will put on this year's show, a much shortened version of *The Nutcracker*. Lara and Ronnie are both Sugarplum Fairies, and Ronnie has told Frank over and over that he needs to take "oodles and oodles" of pictures.

"He'll be there." I'm certain of it because he promised Lara, he promised Ronnie, and he promised me. We've had our rough patches, but Frank and I are doing well now, and I know he loves my family. More than that, I'm positive he'd move heaven and earth so as not to disappoint his grandchildren.

"There you are!"

I look up to see my best friend, Jamie, bounding toward me. I stand up just in time to get caught in a huge hug. An entertainment reporter, she's been in New York for the last two weeks doing celebrity interviews, and it feels great to see her in person, even though we talk almost every day by phone.

"Why are you out here? The food and alcohol's in the kitchen." She's holding a margarita, and it's a testament to Jamie's skill with a cocktail that she didn't spill it down my back.

"Watching the kids," I say truthfully. Then add, in the interest of full disclosure, "and enjoying the fact that Moira is on deck and not us."

"And you wonder why Ryan and I don't have kids

yet." Jamie grins at both of us, then pulls over another chair. She plunks herself down in it, settles back, and takes a long sip through the straw before sighing with pleasure.

Syl and I look at each other, amused. It's barely ten, but margaritas for breakfast is so very, very Jamie.

"You might as well," Jamie says, clearly reading our minds. "It's not like we're driving."

She has a point. Edward, Damien's favorite driver, is coming by with the fleet's longest limo in an hour. It's big enough to fit all of us with room to spare, and the kids will have a blast.

"Well, you've convinced me," Syl says, and I shrug. Why not?

What's better is that we don't even have to get up, because as soon as we've made our decision, Jackson appears with a tray topped with frozen decadence.

"Where are Damien and Ryan?" I ask, taking one, then waving at Lara who's shouting for me to see how high she can swing with Moira pushing her.

"Ryan's making his famous frittata, and Damien's cheering him on."

I glance at Jamie. "Sounds yummy. Is that one of Ryan's skillsets?"

She makes a zipping motion over her mouth. "Let's just say that he is highly adept at all sorts of interesting things. I could tell you, but then I'd have to kill you."

I roll my eyes and turn back to Jackson, who's put the tray on the table. He trades places with Sylvia, then pulls her down onto his lap.

"Is Damien just keeping him company, or are they sneaking in work time?" I ask.

Today was supposed to be a work-free zone, but I know my husband. More specifically, I know the width and breadth of the massive empire he controls, and even during the holidays, work will inevitably sneak in.

I also know that he's good about keeping his word, and when he promises me a no-work day, he'll only break that rule if there's a true crisis.

"Something going on with a security system? Or with hiring a new agent?" I figure both guesses are good. After all, Ryan's been Stark International's Security Chief for years. More recently, he's taken on the role of the head of Stark Security, a newly formed division that is still recruiting agents.

"From what I can gather, yes," Jackson says. "Something about a system breach in an East Asian manufacturing plant. But there's also real cooking going on, so I think you two can cut both your men some slack."

Jamie holds up her hands in self-defense. "Wasn't saying a word."

"Me, neither. Maybe Damien will pick up a cooking tip."

I glance at Syl, who widens her eyes. "Don't look at me. My man doesn't need any slack." She leans back, snuggling against the man in question. "There aren't too many unexpected crises in the world of architecture. If Jackson says he's taking a day off, he usually takes a day off. And I reap the benefit." As if in illustration, she leans forward, snags a margarita, and sighs.

"Show off," Jamie and I say simultaneously, then laugh.

We're still giggly when Damien comes out, his hands in his pockets, his expression tight.

I stand immediately. "Damien? What's wrong?"

"Is it Ryan?" Jamie asks, and he shakes his head, distracted, his eyes locked firmly on me.

"Frank called," he says. "He's not going to make it here by Christmas Eve."

FIVE

I know I shouldn't let it, but the news that Frank isn't going to make it home erases some of the sunshine from the day. I work hard to keep a happy face for the kids, but I can't hide the truth from Damien. And though he says nothing more about it during the brunch, whenever I need him, he's right there, ready to catch me if I fall.

"I'm okay," I whisper before we follow the girls into the limo. "Just disappointed."

"I know," he says, and from the intensity with which he looks at me, I'm certain that he really does know all of it. I'm disappointed, yes. But it's a disappointment laced with lost years and missed opportunities. Of holidays with my cold, harsh mother, who made the season about dressing up and looking festive rather than actually enjoying each other.

Yes, I have wonderful memories of me and my sister managing to sneak in holiday movies and cartoons. But those memories are bittersweet. Ashley's gone now, but my father has magically returned. And in a strange way he has filled a bit of the hole in my heart left by my sister's suicide. And that makes it all the more important that he's here to share his first Christmas with his family.

I know my feelings are legitimate. But I also know I'm overreacting. That the maelstrom in my gut is the product of the heightened emotions of the holidays getting the better of me. But I'd so longed for him to be with us. To move forward through the years with us, sharing the holidays and watching his grandchildren grow up. And I'd wanted to start all of that right now.

"He'd be here if he could," Damien says, squeezing my hand as we sit together on the limo's far back bench.

"I know." I lean against him, safe in his arm around my shoulders. "It's silly, but I had a picture in my head of what this Christmas would be. I'd already come to terms with him being away instead of playing Santa. But to miss the recital and the party and Christmas morning?"

I shrug, trying to act nonchalant. But I'm not nonchalant, and Damien knows it. I'm hugely disappointed. And on top of that, I'm a little annoyed. Because why did he talk to Damien and not me?

Answer? Because he damn well knew I'd be disappointed and he doesn't know how to deal with that. So he punted and talked to Damien instead of his daughter.

But Frank's instinct to evade or bolt when there's hard emotional stuff is the same instinct that pushed him away from me before—his fear that he wouldn't make a good dad—and I'd thought we'd gotten past that.

I'm frustrated, but I'm trying to be understanding instead of angry. Still, I can't help but fear that this accidental physical separation is going to grow into a deliberate emotional one.

Damien understands all of that, I'm sure. Just as he understands that the first step to fixing it all is having Frank here in LA.

And the real hell of the situation for my husband? None of it is something that he can fix. And I know that his inability to make my father magically appear is as frustrating for him as the overall situation is for me.

A few feet in front of us, Moira steps into the limo, pausing long enough to say something to the kids, all four of whom are strapped in near the front. Then she ducks her head and scooches her way toward us.

"Jamie told me that Frank isn't going to make it here for the gala or your party. Will he make it for Christmas?"

I look at Damien, who shakes his head. "It's not looking good."

"What happened?"

"Airline strike," Damien says. "He could rent a car —or buy one, God knows I'll reimburse him—but even that wouldn't get him here in time. He's all the way south, and it's a forty-four hour drive."

"Holy shit."

"Tomorrow's the twenty-third. And he has to sleep."

"Stupid strike," Moira said, a sentiment with which I heartily agreed.

"He'll be here the day after Christmas. The plantation he's doing the shoot for owns a plane. It's in South America right now, but the pilot's due back with it late Christmas Day."

"That's something," Sylvia says. She'd moved from Jackson's side to mine while Damien was talking, and now she takes my hand. "You'll at least see him over the holiday, and he should be home for New Years, right?"

"Absolutely," I say, forcing myself to sound more upbeat than I feel. "I'm just disappointed." I sit up straighter and conjure a smile. "I promise I'll be fine by the time we get to The Domino. A winter wonderland is no place to be melancholy."

"Especially this one," Syl says. As a manager at Stark Real Estate, she was on the committee that put together the weekend event for charity. Remembering that, I double my efforts to be cheerful. Because honestly, it's bad news, yes. But it shouldn't destroy my day. And what holiday isn't without some snafu? I'll call this mine and expect smooth sailing until at least Christmas morning.

"I'm going to go help Jackson with the kids," I say, then kiss Damien's cheek. "I'm fine," I whisper as I pull away.

"Hey," he says, tugging me back. He holds me still, his eyes locked on mine. And then slowly—so deliciously slowly—he bends forward to kiss me. It's soft and sensual and fills me all the way down to my toes.

When I feel as if I'll float away, he breaks the kiss, then pulls back, the corner of his mouth twitching as he says, very simply, "You know I'd fix this if I could."

"I know," I say.

But we both know that he can't.

SIX

"Look, Mama! Snow!"

I turn to find Lara pointing at snowflakes falling around Santa's Workshop, leaving the surrounding area covered in a blanket of white. It's fake snow, of course, but it's actually sticking, thanks to the engineering marvel that is the platform upon which the workshop was built.

"It's not real," Ronnie says, in her most imperious voice. "It hardly never snows in Los Angeles."

"Hardly ever," Sylvia corrects gently. "And just because it doesn't come from the sky doesn't mean it's not fun." She shoots me a quick, amused glance. "Now why don't you take Jeffery and your cousins and go get in line. Aunt Nikki and I will be along in a sec."

Ronnie nods, her dark curls bouncing, then reaches for her little brother's hand. "You can be my assistant," she says to Lara. "You hold on to Anne."

Lara stands tall, then thrusts her hand out to take

Anne's, relishing this responsibility bestowed by the older cousin she adores.

I watch until they're safely in the line, guarded over by a slew of Santa's elves. Then I glance at Syl. "No Santa for us?"

She glances across the open area to where Jackson and Damien stand at a drink cart, waiting for cider. "I already got my Christmas wish. Didn't you?"

I feel the quick stab in my heart about Frank, but I nod. Because she's right. I did. I have. *Damien.* Then, now, always.

I sigh as I think about our girls. "Yeah," I tell her. "I did. My wish—and so much more."

As I'm watching, he catches my eye, then holds up one of the two cups that the stand's attendant has handed to him. I smile in anticipation, both of him coming over and of the warm mug of cider.

"Perfect," I tell Damien. "Especially in this chill."

"Funny," he says, because it's particularly warm today, even by Los Angeles standards. But anyone flying over the scene wouldn't know it. The Domino's entire octagonal courtyard has been transformed as advertised, and now it's a full-blown Winter Wonderland.

Even the little stream that runs though the courtyard is part of the fun, with "icebergs" floating the serpentine path, each topped with an animated character—elves, ice skaters, angels, reindeer, and the like.

The surface area is full of craft and food vendors, but also dotted with a performance area where a local high school choir is singing Christmas carols, several craft tents where kids can make ornaments or work on a variety of presents to give to friends or family, and lots of other areas. There are bouncy houses and games—Lara is desperate to try Toss the Ring on the Reindeer—as well as toddler friendly areas with inflatables and stuffed snowmen for the kids to take home.

"Santa's workshop next?" I ask him. "I want to get some pictures of the girls with Santa other than the official portraits they're selling."

"Absolutely," he says, as we fall in step behind Jackson and Sylvia.

We've just joined the kids in line when I see Ryan waving at Damien from the far side of the fence that surrounds the makeshift North Pole.

Damien's in the process of swinging Anne up onto his shoulders when he sees Ryan, too, and he flashes a wry smile at me. "Be right back," he says, then gallops toward Ryan as Anne squeals and cries, "Horsey, Daddy! More horsey!"

I watch the men long enough to see that both their expressions are serious, but then Lara tugs at my arm to tell me that Ronnie just got a candy cane from a passing elf, and it wouldn't be fair if she didn't get to have one, too. "So can I, please? Pretty please?"

"Yes, you can. And thank you for asking."

Lara beams, and the elf in question holds out a wicker basket full of candy canes.

"'Tis the season," Sylvia says, then taps Ronnie's

nose. "But not for cavities. What are you going to do when we get home?"

"Brush my teeth. Mommy, I *know*."

Sylvia meets my gaze. "Parenting. It's not for the faint of heart."

"It's really not," I agree, right before I hop nimbly over the rope that marks the line. Not because I'm feeling particularly energetic, but so that I can retrieve Anne, who's shimmied down Damien and is making a break for it across the snowy field.

"Gotcha," I say, scooping her up and tickling her as Damien aims a grateful smile my direction. "Come on. We're almost to Santa."

"No," she mumbles then tucks her head on my shoulder and holds on tight.

"No?"

She just shakes her head.

"It's okay. You can stay out here with Mommy." Ashley used to tell me that I was scared of Santa when I was little, too. "In fact, why don't we stay just long enough to take some pictures of your big sister, then you and I will go ride the train while Lara and Ronnie do the big girl stuff?"

"She's not a big girl," Ronnie protests.

"She is by comparison," Sylvia says. "Besides, you two will have a blast, and you know it."

"Okay?" I ask Lara, though I needn't bother. She worships Ronnie.

She nods vigorously, and Anne and I stay until both girls have seen Santa and we've taken so many pictures our phones are probably going to explode. "Is Jeffery going to sit on Santa's lap?"

"He didn't even get as far as Anne. We tried earlier, then gave up. He's off somewhere with Jackson. I'd find him and take him on the train with you two, but I'm going to be a selfish mommy, go find a stand selling wine, and browse some of the vendor booths while the girls are in the craft tents."

As part of the event, all the children's craft tents double as childcare, allowing for much-needed parental recovery time.

"No judgment," I assure her.

I glance toward where Ryan and Damien had been talking, but they're gone, and an unpleasant knot of worry settles in my stomach.

"Nikki?"

I shake it off. "Sorry. Mind wandering. Listen, if you see Evelyn or Ollie, tell them I've been looking for both of them. Jamie, too," I add, even though we had time to talk earlier at brunch and in the limo.

"Will do. I saw Kelsey. I told her that Lara and Ronnie are here and that we're all excited about the show."

A prominent dancer and choreographer, Kelsey Draper also runs a dance studio for children and adults. More than that, she's both a friend and the wife of Wyatt Royce, a photographer who occasionally gives lessons to both me and Sylvia. Kelsey volunteered to choreograph and direct the show, and from what little I know about herding groups of children, I think that qualifies her for sainthood.

"Mommy!" Ronnie runs up to us, Lara right behind her. "Can we go do crafts now? Please, please?"

"Absolutely," she says as I kiss Lara goodbye and elicit a promise to be good for her aunt and the teachers in the tent.

Then Anne and I head off to find the train, and as a bonus find Ollie.

"There's my favorite girl," he says, bending down to pick up Anne without breaking stride as he falls in step beside me.

I hook my arm through his free one as Anne balances on his opposite hip. "I'm so glad to see you."

"Where's your other half? And the other quarter for that matter?"

"Damien's talking business with Ryan." I make a face.

"Crisis at Christmas?" he asks as he buys three tickets for the little train.

"I don't know."

He pauses long enough to take a long, hard look at me. "What's wrong?"

"It's not that big a deal. Well, not the part with Damien. He was a little absent at brunch, but I get it. Things happen. But Frank won't be here for the recital or the party or even Christmas morning. He says he's stuck in Mexico. So I'm just ... I don't know, selfish I guess. I mean, like I said, things happen. I know he's bummed about it, too."

"Do you?"

I sigh as we step into the tiny metal rail car, facing each other. It was made for toddlers, so Ollie holds Anne on his lap.

"And that's why we've stayed friends for so long," I tell him. "You know me so well." Ollie and I grew up together, so he knows me better than anyone except Jamie. And Damien, of course.

"You think that since he left when you were a kid, then didn't offer you a shoulder during the kidnapping, that he's disappearing on you again. Telling himself he doesn't know how to be a dad."

Once again, I shrug.

"He might be. But there is a strike in Mexico, and it's not like he has superpowers. Just because he can't get here doesn't mean that he doesn't want to be here."

"I know all that," I admit. "But I can't help feeling melancholy."

"I get that. But try and cut the guy some slack."

"Fair enough," I say, then reach to take my little girl. "You're lucky," I tell her. "Your Uncle Ollie is a pretty smart guy."

Anne grins and accepts Ollie's high-five with a giggle. She's delighted enough with the train that we end up riding it twice. I don't mind. With his new job at the FBI, Ollie is busier than usual, and with my own business and two little girls, my limited free time is mostly earmarked for Damien. So this is a nice escape for us.

Even so, I'm happy to see Damien waiting for us as

we step off the train. He crouches down, then scoops up Anne when she throws herself into his arms.

"Damien. Good to see you."

"Ollie."

I frown, surprised by the tension in Damien's voice. Ollie and Damien have never been buds—I'm the point of contention between them—but Ollie was a huge help during and after the kidnapping, and the frost between them had mostly melted.

At least, I thought it had.

"What's wrong?" I ask.

"Sorry, Ollie," Damien says. "Do you mind if I speak to my wife alone?"

"Of course," he says, but his eyes look to me for confirmation. I nod, and he leaves, his hands shoved into his pockets and his posture tense.

"What is it?" I ask, moving toward him. "Is this to do with the security breach? Jamie said something about a plant in Asia?"

He hesitates only a moment, then says, "I'm going to need to leave in a couple of hours. I'm so sorry, baby. It can't be helped."

SEVEN

"Seriously?" I snap the moment we're alone again. It's been over an hour since Damien dropped his bombshell, and no way was I going to explode in front of the kids. But now that they're in the kitchen with Gregory getting a quick dinner before an early bedtime, I'm picking up *exactly* where we let off.

"Nikki, baby. Calm down."

"Do *not* tell me to calm down."

We're in our bedroom, the doors closed, and Damien is already opening drawers and pulling things out to pack.

"It's Christmas, Damien. December twenty-second. Little girls. Hot chocolate. Cookies for Santa. *It's a Wonderful Life*. Doesn't that mean anything to you?"

He slams down his toiletry kit, frustration rolling off him in waves. He takes a deep breath, then turns to clutch my shoulders. "Mean anything? Baby it means everything. Don't you know that?"

"How can I when you're leaving?"

He closes his eyes, looking more miserable than I've seen him since Anne was taken.

"Nikki, please. I'll be home in time for the recital. I promise. But there are people—" He hesitates, as if he just can't find the words. "*My* people," he continues. "And I couldn't live with myself if I didn't try to make it right for them for Christmas."

I swallow, my eyes brimming. I imagine assembly-line workers who need whatever crisis this is fixed. Teams gathered to try to avert a crisis, but not able to make it happen without Damien there to make the absolute final call.

And, yes, I know he has people under him. People with power whom he trusts. But at the end of the day, Stark International and all its subsidiaries are his, and that's a responsibility he takes seriously.

More than that, his passion for his work and his skill at building his empire are at the core of who he is, and I can't separate those traits from the man I love.

So, yes, I understand it.

But, dammit, I don't have to like it.

I sniff, then wipe away a runaway tear. "I understand, I do. But how can you say you're going to be back in time? Asia is a really long way away."

He shakes his head. "No, there's a problem in Asia, but it's not the one I have to deal with." He reaches out and cups my cheek, his eyes as soft as his touch. "Sweetheart, this is a fast turn-around. I leave now, I should be home by tomorrow evening. An entire day before Christmas Eve. I know I'm missing out on family time, but you have to trust me. I wouldn't go if it weren't important."

I nod, still feeling miserable, and I watch as he shuts his eyes with relief. When he opens them, I see the fire burning in the amber and black of his irises. Without warning, he pulls me to him, then spins us around so that my back is against the dresser. His mouth crushes mine as my hands find his shoulders. As I open to him. Needing and craving him. Wanting to fix with our bodies whatever has gotten off-kilter between us tonight.

"Nikki," he murmurs, breaking the kiss. His fingers go to the buttons on my blouse, but I push them away, with a shake of my head.

"No," I whisper. Because as much as I want him now, I want him back in time more.

He studies me, his brow furrowed in question. "You're mad," he says, even though I'm certain he knows that's not the truth. Not anymore.

I shake my head. "Not mad. I swear. But I am eager."

"So am I. Or couldn't you tell?"

I reach out to cup his erection, then smile innocently at him. "Shame you don't have time to do something about that."

He laughs, then lunges for me. I squeal and make a leap for the bed, but he's faster and manages to grab me so that we both tumble onto the mattress, him on top of me.

"I could take what I want," he says, his strong arms pinning my wrists down.

My heart pounds in my chest, excitement building. He could—and I so desperately want him to.

"You can't take what I will always give you."

"I'm very glad to hear that, Mrs. Stark."

"But not today."

He hesitates. "You're serious?"

"Kiss me," I say. "Then go. Because I want you back here by Christmas Eve. And then, I promise you, you can take whatever you want, however you want."

He studies my face. "A kiss for the road?"

I nod, eager to get lost in the feel of his lips. But the kiss he brushes over my lips is almost chaste.

"No fair," I protest, making him laugh.

"I'll take the kiss I really want when I get back."

"I look forward to it, Mr. Stark."

He starts to stand, but I pull him to me again. "Damien?"

His smile is gentle. "I'll be back in time. Trust me."

"I do," I assure him. "I trust you to the end of time. It's the world I don't trust. Not any more."

"Oh, baby."

I know he's thinking of Anne's kidnapping, and that wasn't my intent. "I'm okay, really. It's just that this was the second disappointment of the day. I had a picture of how this holiday season would go. And so far it's not working out that way."

He kisses me one more time. "That doesn't mean that it won't in the end."

EIGHT

"We're going to have to make an emergency landing." Grayson's voice blasted over the jet's loudspeaker. "Come up here and get strapped in."

Damien allowed himself one moment of fear before he pushed back from the small table where he'd been working late into the night. This wasn't a crisis. An emergency landing just meant emergency conditions. They were going to come to a stop on the ground, and they were going to walk away.

And soon he'd walk back to Nikki and the girls.

He repeated that over and over, because, goddammit, there was no way that he was missing Christmas. No way that he was going to end up in a twisted piece of metal in Mexico with his family crying for him and Nikki spending the rest of her life wishing she'd tried harder to make him stay.

No way this trip was going to turn out to be a mistake.

"You're tense," Grayson said, as Damien took the co-pilot seat.

"Can't imagine why. What's the situation?"

"Landing gear's jammed."

"Shit."

"I know," the older man said. "But it's nothing we can't handle." Grayson had been Damien's personal pilot for years and was in charge of overseeing the Stark fleet. He'd also taught Damien how to fly, and Damien knew that if Grayson said he could handle it, he meant it.

Still, the man was operating in an unfamiliar craft. This Gulfstream jet wasn't part of Stark International's regular fleet. All the Stark planes had been unavailable, either in for maintenance during the holiday or on the ground at another location. Damien had tasked Ryan to work with Grayson to find a rental, which they'd managed quickly enough.

They hadn't, however, had time to find a crew. So Grayson was flying and Damien was the co-pilot. And the rest of the plane was as empty and silent as a coffin.

As a church, he corrected. As silent as a church.

Christ, he was on edge today.

Then again, why wouldn't he be? He'd left his wife and children—hell, he'd left his heart—to go on a secret mission. Secret only because he'd made the executive decision not to tell Nikki about his plan to retrieve her father by coming to Mexico in a private jet. The idea being to avoid the country's commercial airline pilot and maintenance strike altogether.

Maybe he should have told her. Hell, maybe he'd never know what the right decision was. All he knew was that he wanted to bring Frank home for Christmas. For Nikki. For the girls. For their family.

But he couldn't stand the thought of Nikki getting her hopes up only to have them shattered again. And so he'd stayed silent.

At first, of course, he'd tried to find a pilot already in Mexico or nearby Guatemala who could fly Frank back, but because of the strike, every possible rental had been spoken for. And renting a car wasn't an option since the drive was so long.

He could have sent someone in his place—hell, Ryan had offered—but why ask that of someone else, especially during the holiday? After all, Ryan hadn't seen his wife for two weeks.

Ultimately, Damien had made the decision to come himself. In a jet, the trip there and back was only about ten hours in the air. Even with the additional drive time to and from the plantation where Frank was holed up, they should end up taxiing back to the rental jet's hanger at LAX well before ten on the twenty-third.

Plenty of time, and with all of Christmas Eve still spread out in front of them like a bright, shiny blanket of stars.

This would work. Emergency landing or not, this trip was going to work.

He stayed quiet as Grayson spoke with the tower. But as soon as the pilot rattled off a slew of instructions,

Damien jumped to the tasks, following each to the letter.

Damien was a licensed pilot, and he flew often enough. His skills were sharp, and he wasn't a man who crumpled under pressure. On the contrary, pressure brought out the best in him. And right now, his best meant doing exactly what Grayson said.

Soon enough, they'd dumped most of their fuel, adjusted altitude, brought the plane in toward the assigned runway, and slowed their airspeed.

"Are they ready for us down there?" he asked as the lights of the airport got bigger and bigger in the window.

"They are. TGZ's a solid nest for our bird," Grayson added, referring to the Angel Albino Corzo International Airport in Chiapas, Mexico.

Fortunately, they were making their emergency landing at their expected destination. Unfortunately, Damien still had a five-hour drive through the night to the remote coffee plantation. Assuming that the rental car Ryan had lined up for him was standing by as requested.

Assuming the landing didn't disintegrate into one giant cluster fuck.

None of that.

"Almost there. Almost there." Grayson mumbled the words, more encouragement to himself than information for Damien.

He held his breath, trusting Grayson, but his fingers still itching for the controls, even though his mind knew damn well the right man was making the descent.

Lower and lower, until the buildings became clearer despite the night, and the lights of the runway stretched out in front of them, the ground roaring up to meet them.

This was the moment, and it was Nikki who filled his thoughts. His wife. His children. The risk of fire was real. So was the risk the plane could roll. But if —*when*—they walked away safe, Damien would be even more certain that he'd get Frank home.

Get through tonight, and he could handle anything.

The force of the impact slammed him back in the seat, and he held his breath, his hands clutched on the armrests as he fought the urge to take control. A horrible metallic screeching split his ears, lights flashed outside the windows, and the plane lurched, as if it was trying to rip itself out of Grayson's control.

And then, suddenly, it was over.

For a moment he just sat there imagining Nikki in his arms, her presence soothing him. Centering him.

And then he stood up.

He'd made it to Mexico.

Now he just had to get to his father-in-law.

NINE

Damien woke to the sound of his phone alarm blaring. He snatched it off the passenger seat of the battered, fifteen-year-old Volkswagen Clasico that had been the only vehicle available to rent when they'd finally descended from the jet to the tarmac. Even then, it wasn't an official rental; instead, it was the second car of one of the airport's on-duty firefighters.

He opened the door and stepped out of the car, looking out as rays of light from the rising sun cut through the lush greenery. A small operation, the *Finca de Hermosa* plantation was nestled far from the more well-known and touristy coffee plantations that dotted the western part of the state. Surrounded by verdant hills, the area looked more like a pristine jungle than a plantation.

His body ached from sleeping in the car, but he'd arrived at the plantation gate at just before six after a five-hour drive from the airport. Since that was far too early to bother the residents, he'd pulled off the road, put back the driver's seat, and dozed.

Now his body ached and his eyes felt grainy. But he was here. And unless Frank had missed his message from yesterday and found another way back to LA—and wouldn't that be ironic?—Damien's father-in-law was inside.

It was eight now, and Damien glanced at the display on his phone, hoping to call Frank again, but foiled by the lack of service on his phone. Frustrating, but not surprising. He was far off the beaten path here.

He had some water and snacks in the backseat, and he used one of the bottles to splash water on his face. He imagined he looked like hell, but hopefully not so disreputable they wouldn't let him inside the gates.

He frowned. He'd meant the thought in jest, but the truth was that poverty ran rampant in this area, and it drew drug traffickers like flies, most coming over the border from the south.

Hopefully the trip wouldn't get any rougher than it already was.

After a few quick stretches and a second bottle of water, he felt human again. It was just past eight on December twenty-third, and it was time to get Frank and go home to his family.

The plantation's entrance was marked by a simple but well-tended fence that spread out as far as he could see on either side of the drive leading to the main house. There was no gatehouse, just a rusty intercom that surprised Damien by actually being functional.

Fortunately, his name and meager Spanish vocabulary got him through the front gate, and he walked the short distance to the front door, which opened just as he climbed up the stone stairs to a wide, welcoming porch.

A man stepped out, and Damien's body almost melted with relief at the sight of the familiar weathered face and graying hair. *Frank.*

His father-in-law stood there, his eyes wide with surprise and joy.

"Damien? What the hell, son? For that matter, how the hell?"

"I'm guessing you didn't get my text."

"Haven't had service in days. I called you from the plantation's landline. And the Wi-Fi here is down, too. I've been cut-off since we talked." He cocked his head. "But get in here. You look like you could use some coffee, and there's plenty of that here."

Damien followed him inside where he met Carlos and Juanita Mendoza, the couple who ran the plantation, and whose English was significantly better than Damien's Spanish. "We were just sitting down for coffee when you called from the gate—I shot a few sunrise photos this morning as a thank you to my hosts for letting me stay on a few extra days. Figure they can use the images in their marketing."

"Sounds like I missed a spectacular view by just a few minutes."

Frank didn't seem to hear him. Instead, he simply

stood, shaking his head slowly. "Damn, Damien. I don't think I've been more surprised in my life."

"Good surprise, I hope."

"Hell, yes, but why are you here? Dealing in coffee now?"

"I have a hand in here and there, but don't be coy, Frank. I'm here to take you home. I have your daughter and two little girls who want Grandpa with them for Christmas." He cocked his head, grinning. "Assuming you want to come."

"Home? You know I do. But good God, son. How'd you get all the way down here during the strike?"

"Do you think I'd work as hard as I do if there weren't some benefits to my bankroll?" He grinned as Frank laughed. "Seriously, though, we came by jet." He briefly described the ordeal, watching Frank and the Mendozas' eyes go wide as the story got more and more harrowing.

"After that, I got the rest of the way by car. And, to be honest, we should probably head back to the airport as soon as we can."

He explained how Grayson had stayed behind at the airport to try to beg, steal, borrow or buy another plane. And, miraculously, he'd sent a text about an hour before Damien had arrived at the plantation. Apparently, a Mexican film star had just landed with his girlfriend. And since they were spending the holiday with her family, Grayson arranged to rent the plane for a three-day round trip to LA. By that time, the strike would be over and Grayson could return on a commercial flight, leaving everyone happy.

That was the plan at least, and the sooner they hit the road, the sooner he'd be with his family. More that that, he wanted to call Nikki and tell her that his "work crisis" was going well and he'd be home soon.

"It's a five-hour drive followed by a five-hour flight in their jet," he explained to Frank. "Which means we'll get home at seven if we push it. You might even be able to see the girls before bedtime."

"I'm all for heading out now," Frank said. "I like to leave a lot of lead time. Hell, I thought I was when I booked this job. Never expected a strike."

While Frank gathered his slim bag of clothes and his overstuffed satchel of camera equipment, Damien chatted with their hosts, thanking them for taking such good care of his father-in-law.

Then they were on their way, with Frank in the passenger seat and Damien behind the wheel.

"I'm surprised Nikki didn't come with you," Frank commented. "But I guess she probably didn't want to leave the girls."

"She doesn't know." Damien glanced toward his passenger just long enough to see Frank's brows rise.

"Is that so?"

"She—well, I wanted to see her face light up when she sees you. And watch the kids bowl you over with hugs." What he didn't say was that he hadn't wanted Nikki to be disappointed if he failed.

"She would have appreciated just the thought,"

Frank said, apparently understanding Damien's full motivation. "God knows you do so much for my girl. Hell of a lot more than I ever did."

Damien flashed a wry smile. "I like to think what I do is a bit different. I'm not her father, after all."

"Well, that's a good point," Frank said, his voice laced with amusement. "And I have to say, you two really are good together. I wasn't sure at first. When I learned she'd married you, I mean. All that money—it can mess people up."

Damien thought of his own father. "Yeah. It can."

"You're not messed up."

He smiled. "Everyone is, at least a little. But I'm not messed up that way."

Frank shifted, trying to get comfortable in the small, battered car. "Though you do like your toys. I've seen your garage, my boy."

"True," Damien said. "And yes. I do like my toys. I figure I've earned them."

"Amen to that."

They chatted amiably the rest of the way back, and Damien was pleased when they reached the airport exactly on schedule.

"Should be airborne within the hour," he told Frank as he maneuvered toward the hanger number that Grayson had given him. "And home in time to surprise your granddaughters."

They found the hanger, and they found Grayson waiting for them, sitting in a folding chair inside the cavernous space.

What they didn't find was a plane. The film star had fought with his girlfriend, left her with her family, and stormed back to the airport. Grayson had texted Damien with the bad news, but of course he'd never received the message.

Didn't matter. There wasn't anything he could have done. The plane was gone.

And so was Damien's hope of getting home that day.

TEN

Since the girls and I went to bed ridiculously early, I woke up on this sunny Christmas Eve-Eve before the sun with two little girls and a cat sharing the bed with me. They'd been calm in sleep, their sweet faces like those of cherubs hanging in so many paintings in the Louvre.

Now it's almost three in the afternoon, and I'm having to work hard to keep that image in my head. My sleeping angels have morphed into wild, rambunctious whirling dervishes. On any other day, I'd tell them to calm down. But this is pre-Christmas energy, and I don't have the heart to tell them to stop racing around the third floor's open area, which they've converted into their own version of Santa's workshop, with about four dozen stuffed animals cast as elves.

Except I do draw the line at racing up the stairs.

"But Mommy! It's the North Pole, and we have to fly there in the sleigh with the reindeer."

"Reindeer fly slowly," I tell Lara, grateful that at least she's not trying to drag her sister up the stairs in a colorful cardboard box repurposed as a sleigh. "They have to so they can stop at every house. Plus, Santa likes to be careful. It would be terrible if he had an accident and missed a kid, wouldn't it?"

Lara considers this, then nods. I breathe a sigh of relief.

"So calm down," I say. "And only fifteen more minutes. Then you can watch *Frosty* while I talk with Ms. Evelyn, okay?"

Lara salutes, and they scamper off.

Exactly sixteen minutes later, I've parked them in front of the television, and I'm heading back upstairs to the kitchen. My phone pings in the tone I've assigned to Damien, and it's as if sunshine is bursting through me from nothing more than that familiar sound.

That sunshine turns to rain, however, when I read the actual text.

Baby, I'm sorry. Crisis expanding. Won't be back until late Christmas Day. I love you. I miss you. It's not enough, but no matter what, I am there with you and the girls in spirit. Forgive me?

The thought of his continuing absence is like a knife to my heart, but I roll my shoulders back. Whatever he's having to deal with is obviously bad, and I don't want him worrying about me or feeling guilty.

So I pull up my big girl panties, draw in a breath, and quickly type my reply.

It's never enough unless you're beside me, but we

will be fine. We love you. We miss you. Be safe. I love you, Mr. Stark. Come home soon.

I hit send, hoping that he'll reply quickly. I anticipate the reply, because I know what it will say: *I will. And until then, imagine me, touching you.*

I sigh, smiling despite his absence.

But then *Not delivered* appears beneath my message bubble, and though I try and try to resend, nothing will go through.

My smile morphs into a scowl. A husband who owns a piece of every industry in the world, including telecoms, and I can't get a simple text through? If I weren't feeling so sorry for myself, I might actually find the irony amusing.

The cloak of sadness that's enfolded me loosens a bit when I reach the kitchen and see the pile of Christmas cards from yesterday's mail that Gregory left on the breakfast table. I smile at the colorful envelopes, then frown when I see the familiar looping style of my mother's handwriting.

My chest tightens and for the millionth time that day, I wish Damien was here. Before, I'd simply wanted him. Now, I want his strength.

But he's not here, and I have only myself to rely on.

Get a grip, Nicholas, I think as I draw a breath. Only myself to rely on? Physically, maybe. But that's all. Because even when he's not beside me, Damien is in my heart, helping me find the strength I've had all along.

And that means that I can handle this. My mother and all the baggage that goes along with her.

I steel myself, then pluck the card up with the same distaste I'd show for a nasty tissue left on the floor. I slide the silver letter opener that Gregory used as a paperweight under the flap, then pull out the card.

The image is simple. A line drawing of a Christmas tree. The contents inside are much more complicated.

Nichole.

I know that we did not part well, but I think this rift has gone on long enough. I want to see my granddaughter. Let me know when I can visit, or when you and the little one can come to Texas.

Happy holidays,
Mother

My stomach twists, and I feel sick. *Granddaughter?* Singular? Of course that's what she'd write. Because to my mother, Lara doesn't count at all. And *you and the little one?* As if Damien and our eldest simply don't exist in her world.

Fury rips through me, so powerful and violent I feel physically ill.

What the hell? I mean, seriously. What. The. Hell.

I pace, trying to burn off some of this energy. Craving Damien but knowing I can't have him, and the knowing makes my chest tighten.

I can't even seek comfort with my girls. I'm too upset. Too rattled. And they'd pick up on it. I know their sloppy kisses and snuggly hugs would make me feel better, but this isn't a burden I want them to bear.

Not coming from *that* woman. I want my girls to stay far away from her in every way possible.

The sharp chime of the doorbell pulls me from my thoughts. *Evelyn*, I think, as relief flows through me. Because right then, with the exception of Damien, she really is the person I want to see most in the world.

"Texas!" Evelyn says as I open the door. "I'm so sorry I missed you yesterday. What did my girls think of the Winter Wonderland?"

"They loved it, and they missed you. So did I," I add, ushering her in and through the house to the back patio. She takes a seat by the pool, and I hurry to check on the girls and grab a bottle of wine.

In her late fifties, Evelyn has spent a lifetime in the entertainment industry. She was Damien's agent back when he first started taking endorsements. Now she represents Jamie and any number of our friends. She's smart and strong and doesn't take shit from anyone.

She was one of the first people I met in Los Angeles, and definitely one of my favorites. She's held my hand through trauma and drama, and I'm so glad that she showed up in my life to fill the hole in my heart where my mother should live, but never occupied.

"You're coming to the gala for the Children's Foundation tomorrow, right? Lara is dying for you to see her in her costume."

"I wouldn't miss it," she says. "And I'll bring the girls' presents to your party after." She takes a sip of her wine, then studies me. My whole life I've worn masks. Social Nikki. Beauty Queen Nikki. Science

Nerd Nikki. Evelyn is one of the few people around whom I've truly let down my guard, and I have to fight the urge to hug myself, because I'm certain that she can see the mish-mash of violent emotions roiling inside of me.

"You might as well tell me about it," she says boldly. "Whatever it is, you know you'll feel better."

I can't help it; I laugh. "You really do know me too well."

"Not a chance, Texas. It's not possible to know the people you love too well." She takes another sip. "So spill."

I give her the shorthand version of the story. My sadness that Frank is missing Christmas. My frustration with Damien—that he went away in the first place so close to the holiday and that now he's stuck and not getting back until Christmas day. And, of course, the newest straw on my camel's back—the card from my mother.

"I've got to give it to you, Texas. You definitely have it rough."

I manage a laugh. "Always nice to be validated."

"I miss Frank, too," she says. "And I am definitely sorry that I missed seeing him in a Santa suit."

"Me, too." I take a sip of my wine, thinking about the slow burn that's been growing between Evelyn and my dad. "So, um, how's it going with you two?"

The corners of her eyes crinkle. "A lady never kisses and tells."

"Just knowing there's something you could tell

makes me happy," I say. "Seriously, I hope you two work it out. But no pressure," I add, and we both laugh.

"Between you and me, Texas," she says. "I hope so, too. Who knows? Maybe there will still be mistletoe when he finally does catch that plane."

"I'll make sure of it." I sigh and top off my wine. "Mistletoe. Cookies. Hot chocolate and carolers at the mall. I hate that Damien's missing out on all of that pre-holiday stuff. The little things that are the fabric of family memories, you know?"

"I do. But we both know he loves you and those girls more than anything. But his work—well, that's part of who he is."

"And that's why we love him," I say, clinking the glass she's extended in a toast. "Doesn't mean I don't want him here now."

"I hear you." She sets her glass down, then props her chin on her fist as she looks out over the pool toward the ocean. "Maybe you need to look at this as an opportunity."

"An opportunity?"

"What have you got him for Christmas? That man of ours who's so damn hard to shop for?"

I make a face. "I've got a few things. An engraved watch. Some geeky gadgets he'll get a kick out of. And two signed Isaac Asimov first editions."

"Oh, he'll like that," Evelyn said, knowing as well as I do how much Damien loves science fiction.

"He will," I agree. "I'm still trying to figure out *that* gift, though."

She nods knowingly. "That's what I mean. By *opportunity*," she clarifies, obviously seeing my confusion. "If he's gone for a bit, take advantage of that time. Make something with the girls for him. Something he'll cherish forever."

I nod slowly. "I know what you mean. I just haven't figured out what it is."

She pushes back her chair. "Well, you're in luck, because I have a few ideas. Why don't we go in and see those little girls, and I'll share my ideas with you?"

I stand, too. "I like that plan. Thanks." And for the first time in a lifetime, it feels like I really do have a mom for the holidays.

ELEVEN

"It's not like we had a choice," Frank said, about eight hours after they'd left the airport in the Volkswagen that now belonged to Damien. He'd bought it outright. Under the circumstances, that had been easier than trying to figure out the rental cost and logistics for getting Damien and Frank to Los Angeles in the small car, and then getting the car all the way back to the southern end of Mexico.

Of course, before he'd resorted to acquiring yet another toy for his collection, they'd wasted an hour trying to locate another plane to rent. But they'd ended up running into the same problem they'd had before—with the strike, all available private aircraft had been claimed.

And while their own rental jet was arguably flight-worthy, with the damage to the belly and the length of the flight, Damien wasn't willing to take the risk.

So he'd negotiated to buy the car, and he and Frank

had set off, heading north toward the States and his family.

He'd intended to bring Grayson along, but the pilot had insisted on staying behind. "It's a forty-four hour drive," Grayson had said. "It's going to be Christmas Day before you get back. You go on ahead north. If I can wrangle up parts and mechanics, I might be able to fix our bird. Then I fly to meet you somewhere, and maybe shave a few hours off your travel time."

"Or you could be stranded down here for Christmas."

Grayson waved it off. "Never been much of one for the holidays. Not since I was a kid. No, I'll stay and make sure the repairs are being handled right. With any luck, we'll meet up long before you reach the border. Get you home a little earlier."

Damien had looked at Frank, who'd shrugged. "I guess that's our plan, then."

And they'd set out, but not until Damien had texted Nikki with the bad news.

The text had gone through, but he hadn't heard back. Still hadn't, even though it had been over eight hours since he texted.

He hoped it was the network that was the problem, but he also knew that Nikki hadn't wanted him to leave, and hadn't understood why he was so determined. That was his own fault, since he hadn't told her about Frank, but now with the delay, he feared that he'd inadvertently pushed her away when what he'd wanted to do was pull the entire family closer.

"It will be okay," Frank said, pulling Damien back to the present. "She'll understand."

"I didn't realize I was that obvious."

"I can tell when you're thinking about her. It's one of the reasons I approve of you. I like what I see on your face when you think about my daughter."

Damien managed a smile, but his heart wasn't in it. It was after ten on the night of December twenty-third, and he still had thirty-six hours of drive time staring him in the face. And there wasn't a damn thing he could do to change that.

He was fucking impotent, and that wasn't a state of being that he was used to. It hadn't been for a long time. A very long time.

They drove in silence for a few more hours, both exhausted and dirty. When the gas tank reached the halfway mark, Damien started looking for a station. He'd been filling up regularly since they'd started the journey. This part of the country was remote, with only a few scattered buildings, many looking abandoned. And the last thing he wanted was to run out of gas in the middle of the night in an unfamiliar country.

About an hour later, Frank pointed to a ramshackle gas station surrounded by flat dusty ground illuminated only by the few lights posted above the gas tanks and a tall lamp post that rose up from behind the building.

Damien frowned at it, noting the way the light reflected off of something large and metallic. He couldn't see all of it—just protrusion of metal sticking out past the side of the building—but something about it seemed so familiar.

"Full," Frank said, and Damien turned to see Frank holding the fuel nozzle. "No credit card attachment. Guess we pay inside."

Damien nodded, still distracted, and headed that way, his steps picking up speed as he realized what he'd seen.

A plane. The nose and bit of prop from a small, single-engine plane.

It probably didn't fly. Was probably rusted and engine-less.

But until he could ask the attendant, he could hope. Because right then, the only thing he wanted in the world was his wife and children. And for a few short minutes at least, he was going to hold onto the dream that the small, dust-covered, probably broken-down plane had enough oomph left in it to get him and Frank home to Nikki.

It was the season of miracles, after all. And right then, he could sure use one.

TWELVE

I stand in the middle of the Stark Century Hotel's Grand Ballroom, the venue for the Stark Children's Foundation's Holiday Fundraising Gala, surrounded by bright, beautiful, smiling faces. Women and men dressed to the nines. Children in their holiday best.

The kids are mostly in the far corner where a play area is set up, complete with holiday elves. As for the adults, they're gathered around the silent auction displays, playing roulette or blackjack, indulging in the varied spread of food and drink, or enjoying the band set up by the temporary dance floor.

They're all here to support the foundation, to raise money for the kids that this organization supports, and to watch the children's *Nutcracker* performance that's due to begin in just a few minutes.

As a member of the board and a Stark Youth Advocate, I'm one of the hostesses for the evening, and in that role, I move through the room, my Engaged

Hostess mask firmly in place as I try not to reveal my fears. Because I still haven't heard from Damien, and I can't think of a single reason why he wouldn't be in touch. None of his plants are so remote that cell service isn't available, and as far as I know, all of the countries in which Stark International does business are stable.

I'm hoping that he's simply putting every second toward resolving the crisis, so he's not even taking the extra time to contact me. But no matter how many times I tell myself that, I also know that's not Damien. And the thought makes me spiral down into fear and worry again.

"I'm so impressed by everything this organization does," says a journalist I've met once or twice, but whose name escapes me. "I'd love to interview you and Mr. Stark about its origins and mission." She glances around. "By the way, I haven't seen him this evening. Where is he hiding?"

"Unfortunately, he was called away for an emergency."

"Oh, what a shame."

"Yes, it is." I manage a thin smile. This isn't a conversation I want to be having, and I'm grateful when I see Jamie across the room, signaling me to come over. "I'm so sorry, but it looks like I'm being summoned. Why don't you contact the foundation's press office and we'll see about setting up that interview?"

I make my escape, the tightness in my chest fading the further I get from the conversation.

"How are you holding up?" Jamie asks, and I shake my head.

"It'll be okay, Nicholas. You know it will."

"I'm really worried about him." Tears prick my eyes and it takes a massive effort not to burst into sobs. If we were alone, I would. But I can't lose it now. Not here. Not tonight.

"Hey," Jamie says gently, "he'll be fine. He's Damien Fucking Stark." And despite my fears, I burst out laughing.

"Thanks," I say. Weirdly, that really does make me feel better.

"The gala is incredible," she tells me. "And Ryan and I can't wait to see Lara dance in the show." Her brow furrows. "Where's Anne?"

"Backstage. She didn't want to leave Lara, and Kelsey was sweet enough to agree. She roped some of the older kids into going backstage to help wrangle the dancers, so she has plenty of supervision."

"Nice for you. You can mingle at will."

"Too bad I'm not in the mood to mingle. But duty calls," I add with a shrug of my shoulders. "Want to join me?"

She nods, and we ease our way back into the crowd. "By the way, did you ever get Damien's big gift? Last we talked you hadn't thought of it."

"I did. Evelyn had a great suggestion. The girls and I made him a photo album yesterday." It turned out even better than I expected considering I'd put Lara in charge of decorating the cover of the plain album we'd bought at a craft store. It's covered with family-themed stickers and cutouts of all of our faces, including Sunshine's, and big crayoned letters that say *Daddy's Family*.

Inside the album, Anne and I glued photos to the paper, with Anne adding special stickers to fill in the spaces between.

"That sounds fabulous. He's going to love it."

"I know," I say. And since I don't want to bring the mood down again, I bite my tongue before I can add that I'm afraid we won't have the chance to give it to him. Instead, I ask, "What did you decide on for Ryan?"

"A sex swing," she announces, far too loudly.

"Jamie!" I look around, hoping no one standing nearby is listening to our conversation.

"What? He's going to love it."

"I don't doubt it, but does everyone at the gala need to know?"

She laughs. "You and Damien should get one."

"What makes you think we don't already have one?" Actually, that's a point. I wonder if we do. Our toy collection is wide and varied, and it wouldn't surprise me.

Jamie considers, then shrugs. "I'm just saying ... the album is wonderful and he'll love it. But trust me when I say he'll love this in a completely different way."

I laugh and give her a hug. "There are so many reasons why you are my best friend."

"What can I say? I'm a well-rounded kind of girl. So you'll get it?"

"I'm putting it on my mental list for future presents," I assure her as Ryan approaches. He slides his arm around her waist and kisses her cheek. And just like that, I'm back in the land of melancholy.

"Have you heard anything?" I ask, because other than me, Ryan is who Damien would contact first.

He shakes his head. "I've been trying to contact him, too. No luck."

I nod, my lips pressed together as I once again fight tears. Then I draw in a breath and pull myself together as Kelsey approaches, Anne and Lara beside her. She has a lithe dancer's body and her dark hair is pulled up into a bun.

"Is it time?" I ask, as Anne rushes to me. I scoop her up and she rests her chin on my shoulder, looking out at the world behind me.

"Just about. Are you ready to introduce the show?"

I nod. It's not something I want to do today, but it's one of my obligations. And though Jackson had offered to get up on that stage instead, I'd declined. The SCF is important to me, and I can step away from my worry long enough to tell the guests about the dance scholarships the SCF provides for kids that otherwise couldn't afford to participate.

"Is Daddy here?" Lara asks.

I shake my head. "He had an emergency at work. He's very, very sorry."

Her lower lip trembles. "But he promised."

"I know, baby, but—"

"Daddy!" Anne squeals, and I pat her back, my attention still on Lara.

"I wish Daddy was here, too," I say. "But sometimes—"

"Daddy! Daddy!" This time something in Anne's voice tugs at my heart. I almost stay put, afraid to even hope, but I have to know.

I turn slowly, and there he is. *Damien.* His jaw is scruffy with beard stubble. His jeans are rumpled. And from the look of it, he's been wearing the same white button down for days.

As far as I'm concerned, he's never looked better.

I stand there like an idiot, just staring at him. Just breathing in the fact that he's here and he's whole and he's mine.

"I didn't want to take time to change," he finally says, and the words seem to break the spell. I plop Anne on the ground and rush to him.

"You're here," I say, then repeat it over and over as his arms tighten around me until I can barely breathe and I hope like hell he never lets go. "I didn't think you were going to make it."

"Neither did I."

I pull back to search his face, soaking up the love I see reflected back at me and wondering about what's happened to him. He releases me, and as I step back, I start to ask. But the words die on my lips. Because there, stepping up behind Damien, is my father, looking at least as rumpled as Damien.

"Dad?" My heart twists, and tears flow down my cheeks.

"Hello, sweetheart. Aren't you a sight for sore eyes?"

I look between him and Damien, my mind spinning. "How—?"

But Damien just smiles. "Merry Christmas," he says, holding tight to my hand. "We'll tell you all about it later." He reaches out with his free hand to Lara and Anne, both of whom race toward him.

I step back so that he can squat down and gather our kids to him. He hugs them tight, then looks up at me, though I can barely see him through my tears.

"The full story, I promise. But right now, I think it's time to go watch the show."

THIRTEEN

Damien held Nikki close, never wanting to let her go again. He kept his arm around her waist as they stood in the third floor open area watching as his father-in-law told the story of their adventure to the small group of friends and family who'd come back to the house after the gala for a private holiday celebration.

"So there we are at this gas station in the middle of nowhere with almost forty hours left on our drive. And Damien notices that there's a plane behind the building. Now, I didn't see it, but I guess that something in the dark caught his eye."

"Let me guess," Jackson said, his eyes finding Damien. "My brother bought it."

"You know him too well, but you're getting ahead of the story and stealing my thunder." He aimed a mock scowl at Jackson, making the rest of the group laugh. "So I'm oblivious to the plane. And when I go inside to pay for the gas, Damien circles the building.

And the next thing I know, he's walking in and asking if it could fly. Hell, I didn't even know what he was talking about."

Frank paused for more laughter, then continued. But Damien had stopped listening. He remembered the conversation only too well.

"The Cessna back there," he'd said in broken Spanish, his heart pounding in anticipation. Maybe—just maybe—he'd get home in time. "Does it run?"

The woman nodded, looking at him suspiciously.

"Can I rent it?"

Her brow furrowed.

"Can I buy it?"

She frowned, so after a quick glance at Frank, who simply looked confused, he wrote a check and passed it to her, relieved that he'd had the foresight to bring a checkbook on the trip. "For the plane? Okay?"

She lifted a cowbell and rang it, and a lanky kid of about seventeen had hurried in, looking suspiciously at him.

"I'm trying to buy that plane," Damien explained, relieved to find that the kid's English was better than Damien's Spanish.

The kid inspected the check, his eyes going wide. "This really you? I know this name."

Damien nodded. "It's me. I promise, the check is good."

He said something to his grandmother, nodded, then looked back at Damien.

"It is my grandfather's plane, but he died. It still run, she say."

"Then I'll happily take it off your hands."

"She will do this thing," the kid said, and Damien turned to face Frank, who'd looked as relieved as Damien felt. "But this is too much. Plane old. Much too much."

"It's not," Damien had insisted. "You have no idea how much I want to get home by Christmas. Trust me. It's not too much."

"I—but—"

"Please. You would be doing me an incredible favor. Especially if there are lights for that runway. I really need to get out of here tonight. This minute, actually. And with your grandfather gone, surely your mother can use the help."

"I don't," the kid began, but then shook his head, not turning around to look at his grandmother. "Okay, sure. The plane is yours."

"And *that*," Frank concluded, "is how my son-in-law added an extra toy to his collection."

"And got us both home by Christmas Eve," Damien added, pulling Nikki closer.

"I love that story," Nikki said. "I think that's the third time he's told it, but it still gives me chills. Thank goodness for that boy and his grandmother."

She turned in his arms and cupped his jaw. "Nice and smooth. Although there was something ruggedly appealing about the scruff."

"And itchy," he said. "But if you like it, we can always negotiate."

"I'll take you anyway you want me to have you," she said, then shook her head with a sigh. "I was so worried. And Damien, what if you hadn't landed safely? The landing gear? My God."

She trembled in his arms, and once again he felt the weight of guilt. "I know, baby. Believe me, I know. I thought it would be quick. That we'd be back yesterday. And then there was no service, and—"

He stopped talking when her finger brushed his lip.

"So when you told me that there were people out there—people whose Christmas you wanted to fix—that was us. Me and the girls?"

"Of course."

"Why didn't you just tell me?"

"Maybe I should have. But I didn't want to disappoint you if I failed."

"Have you ever failed?"

He laughed. "You know I have. But I love your confidence in me. And I'll promise you this—I'll never leave again without telling you exactly where I'm going and how I'll be getting there."

"Right now, I'm just glad you're back. It's Christmas Eve, our daughters are safe in their beds, you're beside me, and my father is sharing Christmas with us. No matter what else, I think that this has turned out to be a perfect Christmas."

And to that Damien heartily agreed.

EPILOGUE

I wake to the feel of Damien's mouth on my breast as his hand slides lower and lower, his fingers finding the heat between my legs, stroking and teasing my clit even as he sucks on my nipple. I moan, the glorious sensations pulling me from the peace of sleep into a wild maelstrom of passion.

"Damien," I murmur, spreading my legs and arching my back. I'm not sure how long he's been teasing and touching, but I know that my body's been awake a lot longer than my mind. I'm already wet, already desperate. He's taken me right up to the edge, and I don't even remember the journey.

"Yes," I whisper as his fingers thrust inside me, the angle making the heel of his hand rub my clit in a way that makes me writhe and squirm even more.

His teeth graze my nipple as he lifts his head. He meets my eyes, and though he says nothing, I tremble from the heat I see reflected there.

Slowly, he kisses his way down my body, his tongue lightly teasing my skin, tickling my navel. And then, oh God, his mouth finds my clit.

His hands tighten at my waist, keeping me still, unable to squirm away from any of the sweet torment he is rendering.

My body warms and sparkles ripple across my body. He is relentless, and the pressure inside me grows and grows as all of those sparks seem to come together before exploding outward again, making me see stars as Damien's ministrations rip me into a million tiny bursts of light and joy.

I'm still gasping, trying to come back to earth, when he slides up my body, his weight on me so damn comforting. "Merry Christmas, Mrs. Stark," he says with a self-satisfied grin.

I sigh happily. "If that was my present, I like it very much."

He chuckles, but I see a shadow cross his face.

I don't get the chance to ask though, because of the rising voices outside our door. "Santa came!" Lara cries as the doorknob rattles. I yank the blanket over me, but the door doesn't open.

Damien winks at me. Apparently he realized that the excitement of Christmas would outweigh our privacy rule and had the forethought to lock the door.

"Mommy! Daddy!" Lara's voice is both excited and exasperated. "Come on! Come on!"

"Be right there," I call, then steal one more kiss before getting out of bed.

In no time at all, I'm dressed in pajamas covered with tiny penguins in Santa hats and Damien is wearing a plain gray t-shirt and flannel bottoms with Christmas trees. We head out of the room and into the open area where we find Frank and the girls at the tree. Lara immediately races toward us, Anne at her heels, and thrusts out the present for Damien.

"Me first?"

"Yes, Daddy! Open, open!" Both girls jump up and down, not calming until Damien is on the couch and tugging at the wrapping paper. Soon he has the paper off and the box open. He pushes aside the tissue that covers the album, then sucks in a breath.

Reverently, he pulls the album out of the box, then flips a few pages before looking at the girls. "Did you two make this?"

They nod. "Mommy too," Lara says.

"Well, thank you both. And thank you, Mommy," he adds, looking up at me. "I think this is the best present ever," he adds, and I can tell from the tone of his voice that he means it.

He flips a few more pages, but the girls are too impatient, and soon we're diving headfirst into the ritual of passing out and unwrapping presents. Lots of presents, each one received with squeals of joy.

Even Frank brought presents for the girls. Apparently he'd ordered them from his phone once he and Damien landed, and then he'd called the house to ask Gregory to make sure that the couriered deliveries were wrapped and ready.

Once our exhausted girls are snuggled with their grandfather on the couch, Damien and I head into the kitchen for much-needed coffee. I'm wearing my new necklace, an emerald pendant Damien had designed to match the emerald anklet I wear almost every day.

"I think the girls like their presents," I whisper as we're returning with a tray of coffee, pastries, and orange juice to share.

A huge stone fireplace dominates the center of this room, a focal point at the top of the stairs. As we reach it, Damien pauses, then takes the tray from me and sets it on a nearby table.

"What?" I whisper, and he nods toward the Christmas tree, gently pressing a finger to my lips. I look that direction and smile at the scene—Frank and the girls have moved from the couch. Now they're sitting on the floor, building what looks like a city out of the Legos that Santa brought.

On the coffee table nearby, the album we gave Damien sits. "I love it," he says, nodding that direction. "I'll cherish it forever."

"Good. That was what we hoped."

He brushes a finger over the emerald. "I'm sorry," he says, and I frown, confused.

"What are you talking about? I love it."

"I'm glad. But I'd planned to do more. The necklace is lovely, but I wanted to get you something personal and deeply memorable. I'd planned to spend the twenty-third figuring out what that would be, but then..." He trails off with a shrug. "At any rate, I'm sorry I didn't get more for you for Christmas."

I'm not sure if I want to laugh or cry. "Oh, Damien." I point to Frank and the girls. Then I very softly kiss his cheek. "Don't you know you did that? Damien, you got me the world."

"Christ, Nikki. I don't know if I should frame you or fuck you."

-Please Me

"You're everything to me, Damien. You gave me the world when you gave me you."

-DAMIEN

(Stark Saga novellas):

Happily ever after is just the beginning.
The passion between Damien & Nikki continues.

Take Me

Have Me

Play My Game

Seduce Me

Unwrap Me

Deepest Kiss

Entice Me

Hold Me

Please Me

Indulge Me

Delight Me

Cherish Me

The Steele Books / Stark International:

He was the only man who made her feel alive.
(Damien & Nikki play a significant role)

Say My Name

On My Knees

Under My Skin

Take My Dare (includes short story Steal My Heart)

Stark International Security:

Meet Jamie & Ryan-so hot it sizzles.
(Damien & Nikki make guest appearances)

Tame Me

Tempt Me

Tease Me

S.I.N. Trilogy:
It was wrong for them to be together...
...but harder to stay apart.
(*Damien and Nikki*
Dirtiest Secret
Hottest Mess
Sweetest Taboo

Stand alone books:

Most Wanted:
Three powerful, dangerous men.
Three sensual, seductive women.
Wanted
Heated
Ignited

Stark World:
(*Standalone books set in and around Stark*
International)
Wicked Grind
Wicked Dirty
Wicked Torture
Justify Me

Stark Security:
Charismatic. Dangerous. Sexy as hell.

Meet the elite team of Stark Security.
Shattered With You
Shadows Of You (prequel/short story)
Broken With You
Ruined With You
Wrecked With You

The following series have occasional Stark World Easter eggs

Blackwell-Lyon:
Heat, humor & a hint of danger
Lovely Little Liar
Pretty Little Player
Sexy Little Sinner
Tempting Little Tease

Man of the Month
Who's your man of the month ...?
Down On Me
Hold On Tight
Need You Now
Start Me Up
Get It On
In Your Eyes
Turn Me On
Shake It Up
All Night Long
In Too Deep

Light My Fire
Walk The Line

Man of the Month Box Sets
Winter Heat (books 1-3)
Spring Fling (books 4-6)
Summer Love (books 7-9)
Fall Fantasy (books 10-12)

*Bar Bites: A Man of the Month Cookbook
(by J. Kenner & Suzanne M. Johnson)

ABOUT THE AUTHOR

J. Kenner (aka Julie Kenner) is the *New York Times*, *USA Today*, *Publishers Weekly*, *Wall Street Journal* and #1 International bestselling author of over one hundred novels, novellas and short stories in a variety of genres.

 JK has been praised by *Publishers Weekly* as an author with a "flair for dialogue and eccentric characterizations" and by *RT Bookclub* for having "cornered the market on sinfully attractive, dominant antiheroes and the women who swoon for them." A five-time finalist for Romance Writers of America's prestigious RITA award, JK took home the first RITA trophy awarded in the category of erotic romance in 2014 for her novel, *Claim Me* (book 2 of her Stark Trilogy) and the RITA trophy for *Wicked Dirty* in the same category in 2017.

In her previous career as an attorney, JK worked as a lawyer in Southern California and Texas. She currently lives in Central Texas, with her husband, two daughters, and two rather spastic cats.

Visit her website at www.juliekenner.com to learn more and to connect with JK through social media!

Made in the USA
San Bernardino, CA
01 February 2020

63888555R00104